I0558564

The Prudent Queen

An historical fiction account of Esther, Queen of the Persian Empire

By

Angela W. Buff

Word of His Mouth Publishers
Mooresboro, NC

All Scripture quotations are taken from the **King James Version** of the Bible.

ISBN: 978-0-9856042-9-5
Printed in the United States of America
©2013 Angela W. Buff

Word of His Mouth Publishers
PO Box 256
Mooresboro, NC 28114
704-477-5439
www.wordofhismouth.com

When I think of Queen Esther, I think of a woman who had mastered the mannerisms of exuberating true patience, wisdom, compassion, and the art of being a lady. Her faith in Jehovah and unyielding love for Him was evident to everyone who crossed her path. It seems only fitting that I dedicate this book to two women who worked to teach me these characteristics and who daily displayed a love for God throughout their lives in an effort to instill that love in me as well.

In loving memory of my grandmothers,

Lillian Eleanor Willis Bryant
1928-1984
and
Dona Lee Yancey Walker
1931-2011

Chapter 1
Preparation

Esther peered from the window of the harem which had been home to her for the past ten months. The "Court of the Women" was the way Hegai had termed it, but to Esther, it was the harem just the same. Here she, along with many others like her, had been pampered and pruned, observed and instructed. Just outside her window lay the palace where she would be presented to the king, the sole reason for the sudden change in her life and in her stature. So much had changed in the few, short months she had been brought here. She was the same, yet she was different.

Somehow, she had caught the attention of Hegai, the eunuch who was in charge of preparing the women to meet King Ahasuerus. How, she was not sure, but he had settled his attentions on her. He, himself, had prepped and groomed her, making sure she received the best care, the most fragrant oils during bathing, the freshest meat and vegetables, the finest attire. He taught her the ways of the palace while the other virgins were taught by his predecessors.

Esther had become quite attached to Hegai. In some ways, he reminded her of her dear cousin who had taken her in after the death of her parents so many years ago. The thought of Mordecai brought a stab to her heart. How she missed him. She could almost hear him call to her. Of course, in her thoughts he would be calling her by her former name, Hadassah. She closed her eyes to the memory of the name. Just one of the many things about her which had been changed but would never be forgotten. Esther was a Jew, and though Mordecai had strictly charged her to keep that secret, she knew in her heart who her people were. The royals here had no respect for the Jews—actually, they hated them—but if she were to be chosen as queen, she would be in a position to protect and aid her people for life.

She knew Mordecai had been inquiring after her daily. Though no one knew the familial relationship they shared, it was not uncommon for outsiders to pick their favorites for whom they hoped would become queen. She had seen him walking outside the Court of the Women. He was still looking over her after all these years, and it comforted Esther to see he was continuing to do well, even in her absence. It was also helpful to know that Mordecai was so well thought of among the servants in the palace. It was not unusual for him to be in the presence of the king himself. The thought that she would hopefully see him again soon eased her pain. She may even be able to greet him upon their next meeting—as the new queen of the Persian Empire.

The queen. Although Esther would never be allowed to voice her thoughts, she felt sorry for the king's former wife, Queen Vashti. Everyone who saw her agreed that her beauty was like none other in the kingdom. Many condemned her for the stand she took, but not Esther. She admired the woman. The whole empire knew of the feast King Ahasuerus had called to ready his men for the march against Greece. On the 187th day of this feast, he had called for his queen. The men were in a drunken stupor and the foolish king intended to parade beautiful Vashti in front of them like a concubine. But she had refused to come.

Queen Vashti was of noble descent. She knew what the king asked of her was against the Persian laws. She also knew what he asked was against the laws of God. Upon refusing the king, Vashti was divorced from him and banished from the palace. That had been the end of Vashti's reign. It had also set the stage for the biggest beauty pageant in all the world. No king could be without a queen. Men had begun scouring the empire for beautiful women who could bring honor to the king's court. Upon hearing the news, Mordecai had made sure Esther was noticed and brought to the harem for preparation and her chance to meet the king.

Once King Ahasuerus returned from his terrible defeat, he was more than ready to replace his queen. His ego was bruised, and he intended to find a way to quickly repair it. The past few days had been a whirlwind of bathing, grooming, and preparation. She was not sure when, but Esther knew, because of the recent, endless, treatment she was receiving, that her meeting with the king would be soon. Her thoughts on this were so bittersweet. What woman would not love to become queen of an empire? Of course the thought of endless luxury also meant an end to the common lifestyle with Mordecai, which she had grown to love. Yet, she had no desire at all to become another concubine for the king's whimsical pleasures, which was sure to happen to many of the women here. Only one would achieve the role of queen, a few perhaps cast aside, but many of those she now considered friends would be kept here in the harem. They would be at the king's beck and call whenever the mood struck him, and there was really nothing anyone could do about it. This thought struck an angry cord in Esther's heart, yet, she was mature enough to know the cold, hard truth of the matter. If she was chosen as the queen, perhaps she could change him somewhat.

At any rate, the role of queen would hold a much higher regard in the eyes of the public—not to mention to her own self-worth. It may not be the marriage of her dreams, but it would be a match none-the-less, and a fine match at that. Yes, she would do her best to please the king and win his favor. In doing so, she would assure herself a place in the palace and in a position in which to protect her people. Perhaps, in time, she would even earn the king's admiration and have the marriage she had always desired—a marriage based on love and respect.

"Esther! You'll never believe what I just found out!"

Esther turned as her dearest friend in the harem came bounding through the door. She was so different from the other girls here. Sophia's golden hair bounded in long curls down her back. Her skin was pale and was such a contrast to the other darker-skinned beauties of the region that she was sure to stand out to the king. But it was her crystal eyes that besought everyone who saw her.

Sophia had been forced from her home in Greece to the harem by one of the king's scouts. He had found her hiding and promised her family would be left to live if she promised to do his bidding. Sophia was sent immediately back to the harem. God alone knew if the soldier had kept his promise. Sophia was a resident of the king's palace now. Whether or not she would remain in the harem, or she herself be chosen as the new queen, was yet to be determined.

Esther had fallen in love with Sophia's sweet spirit and gentle countenance. She was lively and fun. She was always ready with a smile, even during the most uncomfortable situations. Her beauty radiated beyond her physical appearance. She was the dearest friend, outside of Mordecai, that Esther had ever had.

"I overheard Hegai talking with that nasty Memucan in the main hall. YOU are to meet the king, Esther! Tomorrow!" Bits of light that looked like diamonds sparkled in Sophia's eyes, and Esther almost chuckled at the expression on her face when she mentioned Memucan. He was the man who had convinced the king to dispose of Vashti and search for a new queen.

"Can you believe it! Months of preparation are about to come to an end! And you, Esther, will be among the first to be presented to the king!"

The breath Esther had been holding came out in the form of a sigh as she turned again to look out the window. The palace was beautiful in the sunset.

"Esther, why do you ignore me? Do you not delight in the anticipation of meeting the king tomorrow? It is, after all, what we have been preparing for these past months."

"Yes, it is." Esther turned from the window and faced her friend. "I would be lying if I said I was not excited with the prospect." Esther stood suddenly and walked away from the window seat where she had been gazing. She looked at her reflection in the full-length glass Hegai had provided for her. It was one of the many "luxuries" she had been given that others had not.

Her olive skin had never been more radiant. Her ebony hair hung long and straight down her back, encircled by a gold band laying loosely on top of her head. She was toned and smelled of rosewater and salts. All of the evidence of the life she had lived before coming here, erased.

"What is it, Esther?" She could see the concern in Sophia's reflection by the way her brow puckered in thought.

"Once the king chooses his queen, what will happen to the other girls here in the harem?" Esther paused and at Sophia's questioning eyes, continued by answering her own question. "They will remain here, Sophia. All of Persia knows of his reputation with women. They will be slaves, forced to do his bidding, for the remainder of their lives. Or at least until he's finished with them. Then what will become of them? Will they be cast out, without a home? Will they be killed?"

Sophia rose from the seat she had taken by the window and walked over to her friend. Placing her hands on Esther's shoulders, she smiled at both of their reflections in the glass.

"That is something you should not be concerned with at this time. We are all here, Esther, because it is the life that has been presented unto us. Some situations you cannot control, and this is one of them. You are the one who is always speaking to us of Jehovah and His plan. You are the one who has allowed us all to cry on your shoulder at one time or another, while comforting us with words of hope from the Scriptures. You are the one, Esther, who helped us to see the good in our situation. We are safe here. Maybe not the ideal situation for some of us, but we are safe and we are kept well. However, I have no doubt in my mind that you will be the one King Ahasuerus will choose as his queen. Upon his first sight of you, his heart will be lost to you and all others will be forgotten. There is not a woman here who does not love you, Esther. Hegai has shown you favor for a reason. There is only one in all of Persia with the sweet and trusting spirit which you possess. Only one who truly deserves the roll of queen. Although any of us would love the chance, we all feel it is you whom the king will choose, and no one here will be angry when that is the case."

Esther turned into her friend's embrace. "If I am chosen tomorrow, Sophia, I will never forget the friend you have been to me. If I have any choice in the matter, it is you whom I will choose as my lady-in-waiting, my right-hand, and if I am not chosen as queen," Esther pulled away to grin into her friend's face, "I will tell you all about the king when I return!" Both women broke the embrace in a fit of laughter. Their merriment was cut short with a brief knock on the door, another luxury the others did not merit, right before it flung open as Hegai hurried through. It was evident by the quick change in his features that Sophia's presence had caught him by surprise.

"Sophia, please return to your chambers." His voice was kind, yet stern.

"Of course, Hegai." Sophia gave Esther's hand a gentle squeeze as she quickly lowered her head and brushed swiftly past the eunuch.

Hegai's eyes never left Esther, as she stood straight and tall before him, no expression showing on her beautiful face. After what seemed like an eternity he spoke.

"It is time, Esther. Make me proud. Tomorrow you will meet the king." He began to walk toward her, proud of her statuesque stance. "What do you desire be given unto you? Jewels? Ornate clothing? Anything you choose to prepare you for your presentation tomorrow is yours."

Suddenly her heart slowed and her mind eased. A peace came over Esther, suppressing her tension and her nerves. She could not explain it. It was just a passing thought, yet she knew it came from a Higher Power. Esther remembered that Jehovah was in control. He knew His plan for her, even if she did not. Mordecai would never ask something of her that he did not believe was a path chosen by God. Hegai continued to circle her as he awaited her answer. Relaxing just a little she turned her face toward him and allowed her eyes to meet his.

"It is your decision, Hegai. Whatever you think will meet the king's approval will be enough. You know what he will desire more than anyone else."

"Very well, Esther, and a very wise decision." Hegai smiled at this woman—this

woman who he was sure would be the future
Queen of Persia.

Chapter 2
Love at First Sight

Esther scanned the interior of the room moving only her eyes. She had thought the colors inside the Court of the Women were brilliant, but these colors inside the palace walls, the deep purples and blues, rich greens and gold, were among the other hues she could not even imagine a name for. All were more vibrant than she had ever imagined a color could be. Hegai was to her right, slightly behind her, yet she felt totally alone in the huge room. She remembered her stature just as the huge doors to her left began to open. Head held high, nose slightly pointed upward, shoulders squared and back as straight as a rod, just as Hegai had taught her. The stance of a queen.

A tall, muscular man, looking to Esther as if he were dressed for battle, emerged quickly from the heavy doors. His face was familiar to her, but his name escaped her memory. That he was on a mission and that he was fairly angry as he barreled through was clear, but suddenly, he stopped short. So quickly, in fact, that Esther almost flinched, but fought the urge and kept her composure. In fact, without even realizing it she tilted her head in his direction and met his eyes with a glare of authority that she did not even realize she possessed.

This woman, this beautiful creature, demanded his full attention. All thoughts as to where he was headed and why he was headed there had flown from his brain the moment he saw her. He had grown familiar with seeing young ladies around the palace who were being brought to meet the king. He was aware the king was searching for his next queen, and he had heard of and even seen some of the recent "contestants" but this...this jewel, was in a league the others could only imagine.

Her skin was lightly tinted, but naturally so, and was the perfect backdrop for the simple, gold jewelry that adorned her neck and wrists. Her hair, black as a raven's wing, was wound tightly upon her head in mounds of braids with a thin gold ribbon woven among them. The ivory gown she wore fell slightly from her slender shoulders and hugged her bodice and waist only slightly enough to show her thin physique, yet would still keep her body hidden from anyone without permission to view it. A brilliant, red cape fell from her shoulders in waves around her ankles. But the key to all this beauty, what really captured his attention, were eyes as deep and as dark as the pools which flowed in the midst of the palace court yard.

Never had he seen a woman so beautiful. Her face held determination, but yet was soft with an innocence that could not be taught. She was genuine. Yes, she had been prepped, but what she possessed was not something that could be learned. She was not here to simply win the king's affection and in doing so, earn the role of queen. She was here to BE the queen.

Hegai cleared his throat and schooled his features to remove the small smile that played at his lips. He was not surprised at Haman's response to Esther. In fact, he was glad that Haman had seen her before King Ahasuerus had. It just proved to Hegai that his intuitions were correct. He had done well with his decision as to how to present Esther. She was, in fact, perfect.

"Hegai," Haman said, a bit too loudly, as he seemed to snap from his trance. He shook his head as if to clear his mind and his voice was gruff, exactly as you imagined a "man of battles" would be. "The king will be with you shortly. We have just finished going over some…" he halted to choose his next words carefully and glanced quickly at the lady in his presence, "battle strategies," he finished slowly. He turned his attention back to Esther.

"And, I apologize for keeping His Majesty from you, My Lady." Haman slightly bowed in front of Esther and reached for her hand. Looking to Hegai for direction, Esther slowly lifted her hand toward Haman. She did not like the way his hand felt as he took hers or the speed in which he took it. He seemed to be enjoying the feel of her skin a bit too much. It sent an unpleasant shiver up her arm.

Keeping her face straight and firm, she gently, yet quickly pulled her hand from his grasp just before his lips brushed the back of it. Haman, in surprise quickly rose from his bowed position and looked at her as though he had been slapped.

Esther resumed her earlier position with her hands cradled together in front of her. "There is no need for apologies to me, Sir. My time is of no importance. I am sure His Majesty will be with me as his time allows."

"Of course," Haman straightened himself and looked taken aback. He motioned his head to Esther's current guardian. "Hegai," he spoke firmly. Looking again at Esther, he gave a curt nod and strode through the room and out the opposite door from whence he came. That she had offended him, was obvious, however, the how was a puzzle to her. She turned to Hegai who spoke in hushed tones before she had time to voice her question.

"Never mind Haman, Esther," He reassured her. "He is well on his way to being the king's second-in-command, but do not concern yourself with him at this time. It is the king you are to focus on. Not Haman." Hegai's instructions were clear. She was to remove the encounter with Haman from her mind. It was the king she was here to impress and no one else.

A noise at the door brought her attention back to the here and now, and before she could blink, she was in the presence of the king. She had often seen his face from his carriage as he went about the city. But he was always surrounded by his armed guards and his face was all she had been able to see. He was taller than she imagined and of medium build. His hair was rather tousled, as if he had been worrying over something, and his face was covered with a rather thin beard. Yet, despite his disheveled look, he was handsome, and his eyes held something Esther could not quite figure. Must be royalty, she thought, and at that thought, she almost laughed at herself. Quickly, she recovered to make it look as if the sight of the king had almost taken her breath and immediately she bowed before him, Hegai doing the same behind her.

King Ahasuerus was breathless himself. This vision of loveliness in front of him was the most beautiful woman he had ever seen. Surely he was in the presence of a goddess. He had worried about having to replace Vashti with someone whose beauty could barely compare to her own, but this woman's beauty far outweighed that which Vashti possessed. Next to this lady, Vashti was merely a "pretty face."

The king schooled himself and walked in the direction of this woman who had left his heart pounding like a mere peasant boy's at only the sight of her. "Hegai, whom have you brought before me?" He stopped directly in front of Esther. The interest in his question and the gleam in his eye caused Hegai to rise from his position and face the king. He knew Ahasuerus would be taken with Esther, but what he witnessed was even better than he had expected. He hoped he had given Esther enough instruction to get her through their first meeting, which at this rate, may be the only meeting necessary.

"Your Majesty, may I present Lady Esther. She was brought to the Court of Women by Mordecai." The king reached out and touched Esther's chin to raise her from her bowed position. For the second time today, a man's touch had sent a chill through her, but this chill, this chill that raced down her spine, was not as unpleasant as she had experienced before. Although it was still slightly uncomfortable, it was not unbearable and Esther did not pull away.

"Esther. What a lovely name, for such a lovely maiden. I hope you have found the palace to your liking."

"Your Majesty, I could not have asked for better treatment or accommodations than what has been provided me. However, none can compare to the beauty within these palace walls." The smile she gave the king was genuine even if it was very shy and small, however, the impact that smile had on the king's heart was enormous.

"Hegai, you are dismissed," The king spoke slowly without removing his gaze from Esther's face. "Esther, come, dine with me. I should like to know you more." With that, the king removed his hand from Esther's chin and offered her his arm. One last glance at Hegai proved to Esther that she was on her own. It was up to her now to win the king's affection using her natural instincts and the things she had been taught by Hegai over the course of the past months.

Her eyes began to fill with tears which she was able to blink back as she watched Hegai bow a final time and turn to walk away from them. She knew that once again, first with Mordecai and now with Hegai, that as she watched this man who had become such an anchor in her life walk away, she was about to walk into a new and unknown chapter of her life.

She smiled into the king's face as she took the arm he offered her. "Thank you, Your Majesty. I would be delighted."

Esther and the king were standing on the balcony outside his private quarters. She had grown quite relaxed in conversation with him. He had finished sharing a story with her of his life growing up in the palace, which had left her in an easy fit of laughter. She was astonished that she could so easily laugh in his presence. He smiled back at her and she was amazed at how handsome his face was when he smiled. She felt like it was a rare occurrence.

"Esther, it should come as no surprise to you that I have grown quite attached to you in a very short amount of time." His smile was gone, though his face was still gentle and his voice had grown quiet, yet firm. He moved closer to her and reached for her hands. Gently, he cradled them within his own. "I do not wish for you to return to the Court of the Women. You will remain here, in the palace with me." Esther looked closely into his face.

"Your Majesty?" she questioned. She searched the depth of his eyes with her own. What she saw there surprised her. Perhaps there was more to this man than simply the blood-thirsty, womanizing king which he had the reputation of being. Perhaps with the right direction and the right spouse he could be much more.

The king slowly lowered his head and gently pressed his lips to hers. It was an extremely gentle kiss, but a kiss nonetheless, and left Esther feeling as though her knees were about to buckle. His next words, however, almost knocked the wind right out of her.

"Esther, my decision is made. You will become my queen."

Chapter 3
Queen Esther

The day of the crowning ceremony was a flourish of events. As quickly as the announcement was made, Esther was whisked into her own private chambers within the palace to be prepared. This time was different from when she remained in the Court of the Women. This time, she was not being prepped and purified to meet the king. She was being prepared to meet her people—as their queen.

She was quickly given choices by servants from what attire she desired to wear, to what oils she would be scented with. Before, all of these decisions had been made for her. It was a lot to contend with in such a short amount of time.

Oh, what she would give for Hegai to come to her and make these decisions again. She still did not know the king very well, but she really did wish to please him. "Hegai. I want to see Hegai." The sound of her voice startled her.

She did not know where the idea had come from or when she had decided to voice it, but suddenly she realized that if she was going to be the queen she would be able to see whomever she chose.

"Yes, My Lady." A portly, older woman turned and walked from the room.

Another servant continued to brush out her hair. Esther let out a small gasp as a thought struck her. "I apologize, My Lady!" the dear woman brushing her hair cried. "I did not realize…"

"No, do not worry!" Esther rushed to calm her. "You did not harm me! I just had a surprising revelation; that is all!" The woman holding the brush breathed a sigh of relief. After a moment passed, she went back to pulling the brush through Esther's hair again, but she did not question her charge. Esther did not notice. Her mind was on the thought that had just crossed her mind. Perhaps soon she would be able to meet with Mordecai. It had been so long since she had spoken to the dear, sweet cousin who had raised her.

She wondered if he had heard the news. Of course he had. The entire kingdom was aware. She smiled at the thought of his joy for her. Then, almost as quickly as her smile began, it faded.

Though she had shared much with King Ahasuerus, and with Hegai for that matter, her heritage had yet to be revealed to anyone. Mordecai had instructed her not to reveal that she was a Jew. Her life, as well as her people's, would be at risk at the revelation. That the Jews chose to worship the one true God was always a problem for any king or nobleman. They seemed to view it as a weakness that the Jews would choose to place Jehovah over them.

Esther knew Mordecai had no doubt that she had kept his commandment to keep her heritage and their relation a secret. She hoped that one day she would be able to reveal this to her husband. She did not want them to have secrets between them. She longed for a relationship with him like her mother had shared with her father. A relationship that was based on love and mutual affection. Of course, her parents had not been royalty, and Esther realized the circumstances were much different. However, she would do as Mordecai had instructed her and hold her tongue. There were times to speak and times to be silent. Now was the time for silence.

Just as the woman at her back begin to wind her hair into a bun at the base of her neck, there was a light knock at the door. Esther continued to be lost in thought, and the knock sounded again. The woman stopped and looked around Esther's head to see her face. Again the knock sounded, just as Esther attempted to turn and see the look of question on the maid's face. "Oh…," she spoke, startled. "Enter."

Hegai stepped inside the door. Esther jumped so quickly from the bench she was seated upon that the maid dropped her hair in a mass of knots down her back. "Hegai! I am so glad you came!" Without thinking, Esther threw herself into the eunuch's arms. She had never been so brazen with him before, but she had never needed to see a familiar face so badly. Hegai graciously accepted the hug and had to keep himself from laughing aloud. He allowed the embrace for only a moment before he pulled himself away from Esther.

"Just look at you," he grimaced as he looked into her face. "You look horrible! This will never do, Esther. Your hair is in a riot down your back and your clothing is atrocious. Where are your jewels? You look not like a queen, but a pauper!"

Esther stepped back and looked down at the simple robe she wore. "Hegai, I do not know what to wear."

Hegai saw her lip begin to tremble and quickly realized what was coming. He also realized he could not allow it. "Then you are fortunate you sent for me." Two claps of his hands brought in a small army. The woman who was originally working with Esther was shooed out the door as Esther was gently guided back to the bench where she had been stationed.

Hegai began ordering his servants to this closet and then another. Garment after garment was held up to Esther's face. Hegai's face was stern, and selections were soon made. Esther stood before the looking glass dressed in full array. Her gown was beautiful. The neckline of the long ivory gown was slightly scooped along her chest and capped her shoulders. Gold was embroidered along the bodice and along the train which began at her waist and then flowed softly behind her. The red cape she had worn when meeting the king, had been replaced by a pale blue one, which she learned was the king's favorite color. This same blue accented the hem of the gown and brushed the floor with each step she took. Hegai had ordered her hair be pulled back from her face, then braided and knotted at the base of her neck.

An ornate necklace was placed upon her chest. The weight of it surprised her as Hegai fastened it securely around her neck. "The queen jewels," he smiled at her. Esther was afraid to touch it, but reached up to it anyway. What seemed like hundreds of diamonds and sapphires sparkled and winked to her from the looking glass.

"It is beautiful, Hegai. I have never seen anything like it," she whispered to him.

"It is not nearly as beautiful as the one who is wearing it," Hegai grinned at her reflection in the mirror. Esther turned quickly to face him.

"Thank you, Hegai. Thank you so much for coming and rescuing me. I was so overwhelmed."

Hegai took her hand in his. "Esther, you will make a wonderful queen. I knew the moment Mordecai brought you to the Court of the Women that I would be wasting my time on the others. Beauty may only run skin-deep, but I know a queen when I see one. There are many beautiful women who remain in the court, but only one with the heart to rule all of Persia, and she is standing before me now."

Esther grinned into his loving face and would have said more, but a knock on the door signaled that the time had come for Esther to appear once again. This time, not only before the king but before the court as well. As she rose from the bench, Hegai stood before her, but this time slightly bowed at her presence as she turned to walk away.

"My Lady." Never had he been so proud.

Esther was not sure what emotions were running through her as she approached the grand hall. King Ahasuerus stood before his throne at the end of the long hallway, which was positioned on a platform above the others. Esther had not seen him in his full royal dress before. The crown upon his head was brilliant but not overbearing. She noticed many of the same diamonds and sapphires sparkling from it that she herself wore upon her neck.

As she slowly began her journey down the hallway, she realized that each step brought her one step closer to the king. Her soft face almost broke into a grin as she passed by Mordecai. It took every ounce of her being not to break her stride. Were it not for the armed guards to the right and left in front of her, she would have run to him and thrown her arms about his neck. She had not imagined he would be among the court this day and have the opportunity to see her crowned queen.

Her joy was somewhat diminished, however, as she passed by Memucan and Haman. That they were standing so near to one another did not seem to be a coincidence. Esther did not like the gleam in their eyes, especially Haman's, as she passed. Unknowingly, she moved slightly closer to her guards.

As the hallway came to an end, her guards exited the procession and left her standing alone before the king. Behind him, nestled on a pillow upon an elaborate column, lay the crown which would soon be placed upon her head. Esther bowed her head before the king as he began to speak.

"Lady Esther," his voice was loud enough to be heard by all in his presence. "You have been chosen this day to become my queen. Will you agree to rule Persia by my side, remaining obedient, trustworthy, and faithful only to me?"

Esther raised her eyes to meet his. "It would be my highest honor, Your Majesty."

The king took the crown from where it rested on the pillow and placed it gently upon Esther's bowed head. Once it was placed securely, the king gently raised her chin, causing her eyes to again meet his. The smile she saw on his face caused her heart to skip a beat.

"Good people of Persia," he spoke again, more flamboyant than before. The king took her hand and led her up onto the platform to join him. He turned her to face her people. "It is my pleasure to present unto you your queen. Queen Esther of Persia!"

Chapter 4
Declaration

The days shortly after her crowning were pure joy for Esther. Not once was she parted from King Ahasuerus' side. Dignitaries and rulers from all over the country arrived at the palace with well wishes and blessings for the new couple. The smile which beamed from Esther's face was genuine. The king doted on his queen every hour of every day. Clearly, his affections toward her were continuing to grow. She enjoyed the way he reached for her hand for no reason or the way he would drop a kiss on her cheek when no one was looking. He constantly admired her beauty and told her so. Esther could tell her affection toward him was beginning to blossom as well.

Because of this, it was no surprise when the king called for a feast to honor his new bride. No one of importance was missing from the massive affair. Never had Esther seen so much food and drink. Dancing and singing ensued and

Esther had never recalled enjoying herself so much, but what she enjoyed most of all was the time she was able to spend with Mordecai.

King Ahasuerus knew Mordecai personally and thanked him time and again for bringing Esther into his palace. Esther was careful to keep the secret of her heritage guarded at all times and made sure to call Mordecai by his given name, instead of by "Cousin" as she had grown up doing. Because of being afraid habits would over-rule her judgment, she was careful not to call out to him very much at all, but instead, stayed close by Mordecai so they could converse easily.

The only moments which robbed the joy from Esther's heart, were the moments she was forced to speak to Haman. She noticed the way he seemed to glare at Mordecai, as though his eyes could cast spears straight through the old man's heart. Why did he seem to hate Mordecai so? Clearly, Mordecai had been nothing but a friend and constant ally to King Ahasuerus. Haman had no need for ill will toward him. She slightly shook her head to dispel her unkind thoughts toward the man. Being tired from all the recent activities must be causing her to imagine things.

Yet, she could not help but also feel as if Haman was using every possible opportunity to be in her presence. Offering to refill her beverage or get her something else to eat, making sure she was not too tired, pointing out this prince or that dignitary. At one point, she felt as if the king was growing tired of Haman's constant advances toward her attention as well.

"You seem to be getting tired, my sweet," the king spoke for Esther's ears alone as the night began to stretch into morning. "What say we call an end to this celebration and retire to our private chambers?"

"I could think of nothing that would make me happier, Your Majesty," she smiled to him. If she only knew what that smile did to her new husband's heart, it would never leave her face.

Taking her hand, he led her to the platform in the center of the large banquet room. "Friends," he spoke and the room silenced immediately, "I trust you have enjoyed yourselves and the opportunity to meet your new queen. I know you have found her as charming and kind a woman as I have. I would like to bid each of you fair and safe travels back to your homes. But before you go, I would like to express my happiness over my marriage to Queen Esther in the form of gifts for each of you. Each of your head servants has been given a gift of luxury for you to enjoy once you return home. In addition to material things, I hereby declare a release to all the provinces in all my lands for one full year from this very day." Cheers went up all over the palace as people realized they were free from the taxes of the land for an entire year.

"Hail King Ahasuerus! Hail Queen Esther!" they began to chant. Waving to the people gathered in the banquet room, Esther and her king dismissed themselves and were escorted to the king's private chambers once again.

As had become their nightly ritual since their first night as husband and wife, Esther sat upon his chaise in her night clothes with King Ahasuerus seated behind her. He pulled the pins from her hair, watched it tumble down her back, and then brushed out the long trusses. "Are you happy, dear wife?" he questioned her tonight.

"I am, Your Majesty," Esther answered him truthfully.

"Then why do you appear so forlorn at this moment?" Esther could hear the concern in his voice.

"I suppose I am only tired, Sire. It has been a very festive day," she answered him truthfully.

"There is nothing else on your mind then? Nothing I can give to you? Just name it, my beautiful Queen, and it is yours."

Esther turned to face him and searched his eyes. She wanted to tell him of her heritage. That Mordecai was her cousin and adoptive father and not just a dear friend. She longed to tell him of the Jehovah whom she served and the peace and prosperity that Jehovah could bring to both the king and to his kingdom if he would but bow to Him. The one true God. But now was not the time. It was the time for silence. She would not go against Mordecai's commandment to keep her heritage a secret. She opted for the other truth at the moment.

"Your Majesty," she began, "when I was brought to the palace for preparation and purification before being presented to you, I made some wonderful friends in the Court of the Women. Hegai was such a help and comfort to me, as were many of the ladies there. I miss those friendships we formed. I would love for them to be able to see the beauty inside the palace. They too were prepared to meet you, and they never received the chance. Though I am so fortunate to have been chosen as your queen, I do feel for their loss in the matter. However," Esther felt as if she should clarify her last statement, "I do not wish that YOU would bring them into THIS part of the palace!"

Esther was shocked at the laugh that burst forth from the king. He rocked back so far that she was afraid he would fall from his perch on the chaise. Just before she became angry thinking he was laughing at her, his laughter began to subside. "My dear, sweet Esther," he laughed. Once he calmed himself and caught his breath, he sweetly took her hands in his and looked deep into her eyes. Still smiling at her, he questioned her. "Esther, do you promise to be an obedient wife and queen to me?"

"In every way possible, My King," she promised him.

"Then I shall be a faithful king and husband to you." His voice was quiet and very sincere. "My reputation with women precedes me, Esther, and has been somewhat exaggerated. However beautiful Vashti may have been, she was never a loving wife. She rarely set foot inside my chambers. Our marriage was an arrangement built on alliances and nothing more." Slowly he leaned forward and kissed her on her forehead. "I anticipate our marriage to be so much more." Once he had assumed his upright position, he turned her back to him once again and resumed brushing out her hair. "First thing tomorrow, you are to go to the head baker and cook, and the three of you shall plan another feast."

"Another feast, Your Highness? But we only cleared our guests from the palace this night. Do you not wish for some solitude?"

"Another feast, my dear. But this feast will be a feast for the virgins. You will have the entire Court of the Women into our palace for a feast like they've never imagined. And from that court, you will hand select your entire force of servants and ladies-in-waiting." Esther turned to him so quickly, that he dropped the brush from her hair.

"Oh, but, Sire, that is not necessary. You do not have to do that. I will be fine, I just... " but before she could finish her broken sentence, he placed his finger over her lips.

"I know I do not have to. I have to do nothing. I am the king. I want to, Esther. I want to do this for you." Slowly he leaned forward and before she could move, not that she wanted to, he removed his finger from her lips and replaced it with his own. It was a very gentle, very sweet kiss. He pulled back only for an instant. Just an instant to look into her eyes and make one last declaration. "And I promise, not to touch a single one of them." Esther was smiling at him as his lips claimed hers once again.

"Now, come with me, My Queen," her surprise was evident as he lifted her easily from her place on the lounge. "I am weary." And with that, he carried her deeper into his chambers and into his room.

Chapter 5
The Virgins' Feast

Esther's excitement over seeing her friends again was evident as each lady made her entrance into the grand hall. Esther was pleased with the way each woman had been granted to dress as they chose, much as if they were still competing for the king's attentions. In truth, a few of them probably were, but it was clear to any and all who saw him, that the king had eyes only for Esther.

The king was impressed that none of the ladies seemed overly jealous that Esther had been chosen as his queen. He was a bit cautious as Esther planned the feast, that perhaps she was more eager to see them, than they her. He knew her intentions were not to gloat over her victory, but he was afraid some of the virgins may have thought otherwise. As it seemed, however, none of the ladies felt that way, but were extremely gracious to her and thankful for her hospitality as they bowed to and were then hugged by their new queen.

King Ahasuerus could not help but notice that Esther seemed to be searching the gathering for someone in particular. He knew her dear old friend Mordecai was there and had made sure she had noticed him. Especially since seeing Mordecai always brought that beautiful smile to her face. He also made sure that she and Hegai had a moment together since she had mentioned him particularly as being a comfort to her when she was first brought to the palace.

But it was not until a fair-haired beauty walked into the room that he saw a light in Esther's eyes which he had yet to see. She was as graceful and elegant as she had ever been, but he had never seen her move so quickly. Esther walked as quickly as was proper across the hall and straight to the open door as soon as the beautiful young woman appeared.

"Sophia," she called to her friend, and at her name, the young lady fell straight to her knees.

"My Queen!" Sophia spoke from her bowed position.

"Rise, Sophia, my dear, dear friend." As soon as Sophia arose, Esther embraced her at once. The king hoped he would merit a response like this from Esther upon his arrival into a room someday. "I have missed you so terribly," Esther spoke to her.

"As I have you, Your Highness," Sophia cried. "I was afraid I would not be able to see you again."

"Nonsense," Esther proclaimed. "Do you not remember what I promised you upon our last meeting together?"

"I fear, I was afraid you might not remember that promise, My Queen."

Esther turned at once to the king. "Your Majesty, if it would please you, I wish for Lady Sophia to become my lady-in-waiting. She was my dearest friend in the Court of the Women, and I cannot imagine anyone I would rather have by my side."

"As you wish, My Queen," the king answered her. "Lady Sophia's things will be brought to your chambers at once. She will remain inside the palace from this moment forward. Men!" he commanded and at once, two chamberlain guards were at his side.

"Sire?" the tallest one bowed to him.

"Bigthan, all of the ladies from the Court of the Women are here at the feast. Please return to the court and gather all of Lady Sophia's personal things. Hegai will accompany you to her quarters there. Take her belongings immediately to Queen Esther's private quarters."

"Yes, Your Highness," Bigthan bowed again before turning his attention to his companion. "Teresh, you shall accompany me," he spoke to a larger man behind him.

"Yes, My Lord," Teresh proclaimed, and at once both men headed in the direction of the Court of the Women with Hegai leading the way.

"Is there anyone else you desire to join you, Queen Esther?" the king asked of her.

"If it is not too much, perhaps Lady Judith and Lady Na'ila may also join my court?" Oh, that smile. She could ask him for his kingdom and he would grant it her.

"As you wish, My Queen." Again the king spoke the simple word, "Men," and two more armed chamberlains joined his side. "Retrieve any personal effects Lady Judith and Lady Na'ila require and bring them also to Queen Esther's quarters," he commanded to the one he called Jamal.

"My King," Jamal bowed to him. Upon rising, he turned to his companion. "Sayyid," Jamal spoke, but Sayyid had re-directed his attention. "Sayyid," Jamal spoke again, but still Sayyid did not change the course of his gaze. Esther turned to see what was so fascinating to the young man and could not help but chuckle. His eyes were fastened on Sophia and upon the realization, Sophia ducked her flaming face from his view.

"Sayyid!" Jamal spoke again, with much more force. Sayyid jerked himself to attention. "We shall do as His Majesty commands and retrieve the effects of Lady Judith and Lady Na'ila from the Court of the Women."

"My Lord," Sayyid choked out. "At once, My King," he bowed and quickly the men marched away.

"I believe the young Sayyid is rather taken with your Lady Sophia. He may be almost as taken with her, as I with you," the King whispered in Esther's ear.

Esther felt her face begin to blush. "It would appear so, My King," she laughed.

"With your permission, My Queen, I shall gather Lady Judith and Lady Na'ila, and we shall bid farewell to those who will remain in the Court of the Women?" Sophia was all but pleading to momentarily remove herself from the royal couple's presence.

"Of course, Lady Sophia. Do not rush yourself. Take your time," the queen dismissed her with a smile and Sophia hurried to the corner where Judith and Na'ila had found themselves.

Esther turned to face her king. "I cannot thank you enough, Your Majesty, for your graciousness in allowing me to have these three women in my court. I have missed female companionship."

King Ahasuerus took her hands and led her to the throne where they would not be approached and he could talk to her without disruption. It helped that he had the foresight to have their thrones moved close together, which was not traditional for the royal couple. In the past, each throne had been placed on opposite sides of the platform, for Vashti refused to allow him to be near her in the all-seeing eyes of the public. She was mortified if he tried to touch her at all if someone might see. The current placement of the thrones allowed him to speak quietly with his current queen and no one could hear.

"My dear," he began, "the past few months have been wonderful and I have enjoyed my time spent with you immensely. I have let my duties await me in hopes that I could get to know you and allow you to know me as well. It is my desire that our marriage be built on a more solid foundation than that which I shared with the former queen. I do not wish for this marriage to fail as my previous one did, Esther." Esther could hear the serious tone in his voice as well as see the expression on his face. "However," he continued, "Haman has brought some things to my attention that cannot be put on hold any longer. I fear the time has come that I must return to my royal duties and be the king I have been appointed to be. I fear I cannot do that and spend the amount of time with you which I have been, as you are far too much a distraction to me when you are near."

Esther was not sure whether the last sentence was to be taken as a compliment or an insult, but either way, it was clear that their "honeymoon" was over. She was quite surprised at the tears which began to fill her eyes. Blinking them back rapidly, she took a deep breath and composed herself. After all, being the queen held particular duties also. "Of course, My King." She was proud at how even her voice sounded

44

although she trembled so inside. "Will you be leaving the palace?"

"No. At this time, I will remain on the palace grounds. And I expect you to come to me each time I call for you. But during the times in-between, perhaps the ladies you have chosen for your court will bring you the companionship you need. I do not wish for you to be lonely."

"Of course, Sire." Esther turned her attention back to the festivities at hand.

"Esther," she looked back to her king, "I will remember the promise I made to you."

Again she looked away before she would allow her tears the chance to spill over. She blinked rapidly, and when she had control she looked back at him and saw that he was continuing to gaze at her. "Thank you, Your Majesty, for the time you have put into our new relationship." Without allowing herself time to change her mind, she reached out and took his hand squeezing it lightly. It did her heart good when he pulled it to his lips and kissed it softly.

Chapter 6
An Evil Plot

Mordecai looked up at the night sky. It was a beautiful night. The stars danced overhead assuring him that Jehovah was still in control and seated on His throne. His precious Esther was the Queen of Persia, and she looked happier than he had ever seen her. He had raised her right; there was hope for their people. He had always tried to follow the will of his God, even when he did not understand it. Praise be to Jehovah, He had blessed them yet again.

"I tell you, we could take him tonight!"

Mordecai heard the hushed, angry whispers and quickly hid himself behind the columns that were near. He knew that voice!

"He is so smitten with his new bride, that he would never expect a thing! We could sneak into his chambers and be done with it!"

It was Bigthan and Teresh, chief guards of the king! Mordecai held his breath and eased deeper into the shadows so he would not be found out.

"Patience, Teresh. I too grow tired of the king's so-called ruling. He worries more about his parties and his women than the good of his kingdom. We would have taken Greece had it not been for his recent divorce of Queen Vashti."

"He was never man enough for her anyway."

"Agreed, and I agree to the need to be rid of him, but in due time, Teresh. Rushing into it will only get us caught. We should wait until he tires of his bride and returns to ruling his country. Once his bed consists of only him, we have a better chance of not being caught. If she wakes as we kill him, what are we to do? Kill her too?"

"I have no argument with the queen! Why waste a pretty face? But if we wait until he begins making decisions regarding the kingdom again, we just risk that much more. Once his decrees are signed, there is no reversing them! Think of it, Bigthan. This could all be over come morning."

"I do not know, Teresh. The palace is full of the virgins this night. I fear there will be too many eyes in too many places."

"No more than are usual once the king retires to his quarters! After all, it is we who guard the door this night. No one else will be the wiser. And, if we blind-fold the queen first, she will not be able to identify us."

"You make a good point, Teresh. It would be nice to have it over with. Ok. Tonight.

We'll do it tonight once the king and queen retire. No more talk about it! Someone is approaching."

"Bigthan! Teresh!" It was Jamal and Sayyid returning from their task. "I was just giving Sayyid here grief over being so smitten with the queen's new lady-in-waiting, Lady Sophia." As Jamal dramatically quoted her name, he laid his hands over his heart. "He about lost his head before he had a chance to win her heart!" The men laughed and joked at the expense of the younger man.

"Laugh if you will," Sayyid argued at them. "We shall see who is the last to laugh when I win the fair maiden's hand, and you have only yourselves for company."

"Ah, youth." Jamal popped his friend on the back. "Come, my young friend. We shall give you some instructions on wooing your love." The men continued on their way jesting their young friend.

Mordecai waited until he was sure the men had gone back through the palace doors before he slipped from his hiding place. He had to get word to Esther and the king immediately. It was almost time for the feast to end and they would be returning to their chambers. How quickly his peace of the evening had been robbed. He knew the men were first going to the queen's chambers to deliver the items they had retrieved. He may still be able to catch the royal couple in the banquet hall.

Quickly he ran up the steps and through the same doors into the palace that the would-be assassins had just used. He did not wish to alarm the entire palace, but he had to get to the king and queen before Bigthan and Teresh returned. As Mordecai entered the banquet hall, his eyes frantically searched the rooms for signs of Esther or the king. The thrones sat empty and the rooms had begun to clear. All evidence that the royal couple had retired for the evening.

No, no, no! This could not happen! Mordecai searched through the palace halls, knowing there was no way he could keep silent with the news he had just heard, but not knowing how to get the news to the king and queen if they were already in the king's private quarters. No one was allowed there, under any circumstances, besides the chief guards, and tonight, they would be the very threat to the king they were supposed to be protecting him from.

Mordecai ran as fast as he could through the palace halls. As he grew closer to the king's quarters, he thought he could hear Esther's sweet laughter drifting through the air. The happiness he had witnessed radiating from her face in the recent weeks pushed his old feet forward. He could not let her be robbed of her happiness so quickly or allow the king to die unjustly.

Just as he rounded the final corner that led into the royal couple's private chambers, Mordecai heard what he had been trying so hard to prevent. The click of the closing door. He slowed to a stop and stared at the closed portal. He had been so close to them, yet had missed them. But he could not give up. He would not! He had to get word to them.

"Oh, Jehovah!" Mordecai cried. "What am I to do? Show me, my God! Direct my path!" Mordecai fell to his knees in the middle of the hall and was so engrossed in his prayers and his pleadings that he did not hear when the door opened once again.

"Mordecai!" Esther cried! She fell to her knees beside him. "Dear Cousin," she whispered. "Whatever is wrong?" She ran her hands along both sides of his face, trying to determine if he was in pain or if he had gone mad. Her guards were two paces behind her, wondering if they should intervene and remove the old man or let them be.

"My Queen, My Queen," Mordecai cried. "I come with news." Mordecai tried to calm the beating of his frantic heart. "Where is the king?" His breathing was labored and Esther feared his heart would give way and he would die there in her arms.

"He is in his chambers. I am to return to my own chambers this night to join my court. Dear, Mordecai, whatever has you in this horrid state?" They were both still crumpled in the palace floor, her arms still around him.

Mordecai worked to control his breathing so that he could speak quickly and clearly. "I overheard Bigthan and Teresh, out in the courtyard, just inside the king's gate. They are planning to assassinate the king. Tonight! In his chambers, as he sleeps. They are plotting to kill him, My Queen. They want him dead!" Mordecai breathed easier once his news had been delivered.

Esther looked to the guards behind her. Immediately, two of them, Yusuf and Hasan, turned and rushed back through the door.

Esther returned her attention to her cousin. "Mordecai, are you sure it was Bigthan and Teresh? They are his chief chamberlains!"

"Yes, Esther, I am sure. I heard their voices and saw their faces as clear as I see and hear you now."

"You have done well. I will make sure the king knows of your allegiance. Now, please, calm yourself before illness befalls you. Tomer, please accompany dear Mordecai to a chamber for the night where he may rest comfortably here in the palace." Esther gave Mordecai a parting hug and rose to her feet.

"Yes, My Queen" her guard bowed to her. He then reached for Mordecai's arm and assisted him in rising. "I will care for him myself, My Lady."

"Thank you, Tomer." Esther turned to her remaining guards. Without a word, they returned together through the doors which led to the king's quarters. Yusuf and Hasan were standing at arms outside his room.

"No one has entered nor exited, My Lady," Yusuf reported.

"Have you told the king of the news?" she questioned him.

"No, My Queen. We wanted to make sure you felt it was accurate before we alarmed the king."

"Thank you, Yusuf." Pausing only momentarily, Esther raised her hand to knock at the door. She was not sure how she would be taken. The king had not entirely dismissed her for the evening. As a matter of fact, she could not quite remember why she had exited his chambers to begin with, besides the overwhelming urge she was needed outside the doors. To her relief, before she could knock, the door opened and the king stood before her.

"There you are, My Queen. I wondered what had become of you so quickly. Esther, your face has lost all color. Are you ill?" The king reached to stable her.

"Your Majesty, I have some terrible news," Esther began quickly as he led her into his room.

"Yes, my dear. What is it?" The king noticed her shaking and pulled her into a gentle embrace. "My Queen, what has troubled you so?"

Esther pulled herself back from his arms and looked into his face. "Mordecai was in the hallway, just outside the door to your chambers. He gave me disturbing news. My King, an assassination has been planned for tonight. Yours! And by the very hands of those you completely trust, Bigthan and Teresh!"

The king released her and looked into her face as if she had taken leave of her senses.

"I know how this sounds, Your Majesty, but Mordecai has no need to fabricate such a story. He overheard them in the courtyard as they returned from gathering my ladies' things from the Court of the Women. They plan to kill you this night as you sleep!"

Two claps of the king's hands brought a small army into his room. "Sayyid! You will take the queen to her private quarters, and you will not leave her side! Do you understand?"

"Clearly, Your Majesty!" Sayyid came to stand directly by Esther. "My Queen, you will accompany me willingly?" he questioned her.

"Of course," she answered him, worried as to what steps he might take otherwise. The king kissed her softly on the cheek.

"Go now, my dear. I will get to the bottom of this accusation, and I do not want you present for it."

It seemed like days had past, but in actuality it was but a few hours before the king sent word for Esther to join him once again. She hurried to his chambers for fear of what to expect and for fear of keeping him waiting. While the investigation had been going on, she had spent a bit of time checking on Mordecai and the rest of the time in fervent prayer.

Welcoming the king's embrace upon seeing him again, she rested in the fact that Bigthan and Teresh had indeed been convicted of treason and of planning to assassinate the king. Mordecai had indeed saved his life, and that was not a fact the king had taken lightly. Immediately after he had sentenced the two men to be hanged for their crimes, he had sent for his recorder to record the heroics of Mordecai in the Chronicles.

"You will stay with me tonight, Esther. We will part tomorrow," he told her as he held her. But tonight was different than all others of the past weeks. Tonight instead of talking at length, brushing through her hair, and enjoying one another before they retired, the king simply held her in his arms as they each drifted off to sleep.

Chapter 7
A Surprise Promotion

The morning after the attempted assassination had come all too quickly for Esther. The king had walked her to her chambers after they broke the fast together, kissed her gently, and promised he would call for her once important decisions regarding his kingdom had been made. That had been two weeks ago.

At first, Esther had busied herself by catching up with the ladies of her court. She had missed their light banter and easy laughter in the months since she had become a bride. Esther was pleased with her selection of the ladies, especially her chosen lady-in-waiting, Lady Sophia. Her friend was proving as dear to her in the palace as she was when they remained in the Court of the Women. It came as no surprise that Sayyid was the main chamberlain to guard the door to the queen's quarters. Sophia continued to blush each time she passed by him but seemed to search out every opportunity to do so.

It was on the second day of the second week of her solitude that Esther decided to expand her horizons. Although there was plenty to entertain her in her expansive quarters, she longed to see faces other than her court and to breathe in some fresh air. Perhaps she would see the face she longed for as she moved about the palace, as well.

With Sophia, Judith, and Na'ila accompanying her, the queen and her court left her chambers to stretch their legs in the late afternoon sun. How wonderful it felt on their skin. Esther was enjoying a moment alone, as alone as a queen could be with constant body-guards, admiring a peculiar color of rose winding its way up the trellis along her path, when she noticed her guards bow to someone behind her. Her heart skipped a beat.

Her brightest smile lit her face as she turned prepared to see her king. That smile did not linger.

"Haman?" Esther could not cover the surprise in her voice. She turned back to her guards. "Why do you bow to Haman, Tomer?" she asked him directly.

"My Queen, Our Highness the King, recently promoted Master Haman to Prime Minister." Tomer could not miss the moment of shock that crossed his queen's face. "He is second-in-command, My Lady. Second only to the king," Tomer explained to her patiently.

Esther continued to gage Tomer's serious expression. She knew it was out of character for him, but she half expected him to dissolve into laughter at his own joke. When his expression failed to change, Esther knew he was, in fact, very serious.

"Of, of course….." Esther struggled for something positive to say, but could find nothing.

"My Lady, My…Queen." Haman bowed to her slowly. His tone was sarcastic and made Esther's skin crawl. But never would she allow him to see her disgust toward him.

"It seems congratulations are in order, Haman," Esther ducked her head in his direction in return. "Was there an act of some kind that caused this promotion?"

"It has always been my pleasure, as well as my family's before me, to serve this land, and my king as prominently as I know how. His Majesty only felt it beneficial to promote me for my years of service and dedication to the crown."

You mean for your years of deceit and dedication of finding a way to steal the crown? Esther thought to herself, but instead opted for, "I am sure His Majesty has made a choice he feels will be very beneficial to our kingdom."

Haman reached for her hand, at the same moment Sophia called for her.

"My Lady! You simply must see the roses!" she interrupted them. "Oh! I do apologize, Master Haman," Sophia bowed before him. "I did not realize you had joined our queen in the gardens."

"No harm done, Sophia!" Esther quickly defended her lady-in-waiting. "Haman was just passing through the gardens himself." Esther smiled back at him, her hands never leaving her side. "Good day, Haman." The two ladies turned to walk away but turned at Haman's next words.

"Have you been fortunate enough to see His Majesty as of late, My Lady?"

It took everything Esther could muster not to turn on him at those words. She knew he was fishing for something to take back to the king. A temper-tantrum, a hint that she was passing her time with another and could care less for him. Anything he could twist and turn into something other than what she actually said. An earlier confrontation with Haman was brought quickly to her mind.

"As I have told on another occasion, Haman," she spoke to him sweetly, "my time is of no importance. I am sure the king will send for me as his time allows."

"Indeed, My Lady," Haman bowed to her. But she did not miss the smirk on his face as she turned to walk away.

"Please do not worry, My Queen. I am sure His Majesty will call for you very soon. Perhaps advancing Master Haman was the decision he was struggling with. Now that it has been done, I am sure you will hear from him very shortly," Sophia was trying to reassure her queen.

"If it is of any consolation, My Lady, His Majesty has not been observed near nor has he summoned anyone from the Court of the Women," Na'ila added.

"Na'ila," Esther spoke firmly, "it will not be your habit to keep up with the king's visits to or from the Court of the Women. I appreciate your concern in my distress, but I have no reason to doubt the king's fidelity to me."

"Of course not, My Queen. Please accept my utmost apology." Na'ila bowed to her queen. "Please excuse me, Your Highness."

Esther would never admit it, but that realization did ease a weight from her shoulders. She hoped she had not been too harsh with Na'ila, but she did not like the idea of anyone "keeping tabs" on their personal affairs.

A knock was heard at that moment at the entry way to the queen's chambers. Esther rose from her place on her lounge. "Enter," she called kindly.

"My Lady," Yonatan, one of the king's chamberlains, bowed before her as soon as Judith opened the door. "His Majesty, King Ahasuerus, requests your presence in his quarters within the hour."

"Please tell the king I will be there straight away," Esther answered.

"As you wish, My Queen," Yonatan bowed again and exited the room.

Before the door was closed securely behind him, Sophia, as well as Judith and Na'ila, were everywhere, grabbing brushes, combs and scented oils.

"Come, My Queen!" Sophia smiled as she began pulling garments from the queen's vast wardrobe. "We must ready you immediately! Get that green off! Although the color looks beautiful on you, I do believe I remember hearing you mention the king's favorite color is blue!" Esther could not help but laugh as Sophia stood there holding up a beautiful blue gown.

Esther was nestled securely on the king's arm. He was absent mindedly playing with a lock of her hair. "I have missed you, My Queen," Ahasuerus said quietly.

"As I have you," Esther answered him. "I was about to believe you had forgotten I was here." Though the comment was made lightly, it held a bit of truth and the king recognized it immediately.

The king positioned her so that he could look into her eyes. "I will be busy from time to time, and spans of time may pass that seem as if you are forgotten, but nothing could be farther from the truth, Esther. Though you may not be present in my arms continually, you are always present in my heart."

Esther could not believe the sentiment radiating from the king at this moment. She had seen the fire of battle in his eyes as he and his men had ridden through the city in their failed quest to conquer Greece. That had been before she knew him as she did now. She had seen defeat in his eyes when he returned from that very battle. She had seen interest in his eyes the day they had first actually met, and then again on the day she officially became his queen. She had seen fear in his eyes the night they were trying to get to the bottom of the planned assassination—fear for her life as well as his own. But what she was seeing now was something different. This may very well be love.

He leaned down until his lips touched her own and gently kissed her. "I will try not to allow my business transactions to interfere with our relationship for very long periods of time; however, sometimes it simply cannot be helped." He seemed to be apologizing to her.

"Do not let it concern you, My King," Esther reached up to rub the stubble on his face. "I am content in your absence, though I long for your presence. We are together now, and that is what matters"

"You are so good for me, Esther," he proclaimed as he nestled her back into his arms. "Is there anything you wish for? Anything I can get for you? Just name it and it shall be yours."

Esther thought about the secret she had kept hidden from him all this time. Was now the moment she should share her Jewish heritage with him, to bear her soul of who Mordecai really was? Should she tell him the fear that stabbed her heart at the very sight of Haman, for reasons she could not quite identify?

No. It still was not the time. Now was the time for silence.

"With you here with me, I have all I need, Your Majesty," she answered him honestly. Then with a comfortable sigh, she nestled deeper into his arms and closed her eyes to sleep. Neither of them would have slept so soundly, however, if they could have realized just how much his "business transactions" were about to impact their relationship.

Chapter 8
Haman the Magnificent

How Haman loved this time of day, or any time of day that he strolled through the streets of the city. Actually, he took any opportunity possible to do so. Now that he was the king's second-in-command, he received admiration from the people just as the king did. As Haman approached, people fell to the dirt on their faces to worship the very ground he walked on.

"Bow! Bow I say! Prime Minister Haman approaches!" his chamberlain would shout and the people would immediately drop to the earth. He almost laughed out loud as he watched men, women, and children stumble all over themselves in order to bow before he passed by them.

This is what Haman desired. Worship. The worship that was due him. He was, after all, a descendent of King Agag. That was something he was secretly very proud of. His people had survived destruction centuries ago at the hands of King Saul and the country of Israel. His ancestors had vowed to wash the filthy Jews from the land and in doing so, purge the land of the God they claimed to worship. No God that could not be seen deserved worship, especially when he was here in their very presence. But instead of his people destroying the Jews, the Jews had in fact revolted and almost destroyed them. Of course, they had not quite succeeded, or he would not be here today.

Oh, how he hated the Jewish people—filthy, insolent, infidels claiming to worship the only, one, true God. If he could find a way, and he would, Haman would lead a revolt and wash the streets of Persia with the blood of the Jews.

Haman strolled through the king's gates toward his own home. Perhaps he should surprise his wife, Zeresh, to see how she was passing her day as "the wife of the Prime Minister." Oh how that title suited Haman. He chuckled to himself as his chamberlain stopped right outside his door to allow him to enter.

"Zeresh! Zeresh!" Haman bellowed as he entered his home. "Where are you, woman?"

"I am here, Haman. Why do you call for me now? It is not yet time for you to return home!" she yelled back to him from her place lounging on a piece of exquisite furniture. One of their newly acquired servants stood behind her, fan in one hand, a plate of grapes in the other.

"Is this what you have done all day? Lounge around, eating grapes, acting as though you have nothing more than time on your hands?" Haman walked in and plopped onto the lounge beside his wife.

"What else is there to do?" she smiled to him as she stifled a yawn. "Now that you have been promoted to Prime Minister, I have nothing to concern me except finding creative ways to pass the time!" They both laughed at the half-hearted joke.

"I tell you, Zeresh. I may not wear the crown, but in due time, I shall control it. It was much easier than I expected to convince the king I should be his second-in-command. Just think of it, Zeresh, all I had to do was suggest a promotion on my behalf and the king made it so. The House of Haman is sure to rise once again!"

"Oh, yes, Haman. Your dear old ancestor, King Agag, would be so proud of you." Zeresh repositioned herself on the lounge to draw closer to Haman. "Of course, I am as well." Zeresh toyed with the goblet she held in her hand and cast her brown eyes toward her husband. "However, there is talk that some of the locals are displeased with your advancement in rank."

"What? What nonsense is this? Where have you heard such?" Haman snapped his fingers to signal a servant. "How is it," he barked as the small man approached, "that I have been sitting in my home for a full five minutes and do not yet have a drink in my hand?"

"Of course, My Lord! I do apologize!"

"Memucan was here earlier today." Zeresh looked to see how Haman would accept the news that Memucan had visited unannounced. "He told me that he had observed a certain man refusing to bow as you passed through the city." Zeresh took a sip from her goblet, then handed it off to her own servant. With a wave of her hand, she dismissed him from her presence. "I am sick of looking at him today," she smiled to her husband.

"Memucan was here? What was the purpose of his visit?" Haman begin to take long drinks from the goblet he had just acquired. Zeresh picked up the hint of jealousy in his voice.

"Oh, he came looking for you, my dear," she covered sweetly. "He was just concerned that if one man gets by without bowing as you pass, that others may see and feel they also have the option to openly disrespect you." Zeresh batted her eyes at her husband.

"If there is one in this city who dares disrespect me, he will pay with his life."

"It seems when this man was questioned," here she paused to give Haman time to look to her. Once she knew she had his undivided attention, she continued slowly, "he claimed he would worship only the one….true….God." Zeresh allowed the words to sink in. Upon realizing what his wife was implying, Haman surprised her by bolting straight off the lounge. "Haman! Where are you going?" Fear was evident in her face, for she knew her husband's temper and was not sure of the direction his anger would take him.

"A Jew! A Jew in Persia who dares defy me!" Haman's goblet shattered against the wall, the contents forgotten. "I will walk through this city all night if I have to! I will find the man who dares not bow before me! I am Haman, THE Prime Minister of Persia! No one will defy me, Zeresh! No one I tell you!" Haman jerked opened the door and stormed out into the streets. He would find out who was openly rebuking the king's orders by refusing to bow to him. And he knew where to look first.

Once the dust begin to settle, Memucan stepped from his hiding place behind the curtain. "Well, that went well," he smiled to Zeresh.

"As I knew it would. I told you Memucan. You underestimate me. I will find a way to exalt my family. Haman is a good man and a good husband; he just needs a little subtle persuasion from time to time." Zeresh made herself comfortable on the lounge once again.

"And that is something you have never had an ounce of trouble with, is it Zeresh? Persuasion, I mean? Indeed it was your idea to rid the king of his previous queen. So, in order to achieve that goal, you merely mentioned to me how much better off the king would fight in Greece if he were angry about the loss of his wife back home. You assumed he would channel that anger into rage and destroy anyone in his path." Memucan advanced toward her. "Was that a ploy, Zeresh? Or did you hope that once his temper cooled, the king would be so distraught over the divorce of his wife, that he would make a careless mistake, and that would cause his life to end at the hands of the Greeks?"

"Memucan, how dare you accuse me of such wickedness! It was your idea to suggest the king have Vashti dance during that feast! It was also your idea to suggest the king be rid of her once she refused to do his bidding! Do not try to point your crooked finger at me," Zeresh was back on her feet and in his face.

"Ah, but now the king has a new queen and has never been so happy. So happy in fact that he's quite careless in whom he trusts with his kingdom and when. So that was your ploy then, Lady Zeresh? Because King Ahasuerus failed to lose his life in Greece, thereby opening the throne to someone easier to control, have him lose his heart instead?"

Memucan had come full circle around her and spoke quietly over her shoulder. Zeresh turned to look at him.

"A woman never reveals her secrets," she answered him smoothly. "Now, if you will excuse me, Memucan. My husband is sure to return home soon, and I doubt he will be in the mood for company this night."

"Of course, My Lady. Until we find a need to 'plot' again." Memucan bowed to her and turned to show himself to the door.

"Memucan," his name on her lips stopped him in his tracks. He turned to her again and saw a determined look in her eyes. "My husband will prevail. The house of Haman will rise again. I will see to that."

"Of this I am sure, My Lady. Once you put your mind to something, there is nothing you cannot achieve."

Mordecai was propped against a column just outside the king's gate. The conversation he was holding with one of the king's servants was not heated, but was not a pleasant one by any means.

"Mordecai, it is the king's command that all men bow to Haman. We do not have to like him, but we must bow to him in any case. You bow before the king with no hesitation, do you not?"

"Ja'al, I have no problem bowing in respect for the king. What I have a problem with is that it is not respect which Haman demands. It is worship. I will worship none, except the one, true God." Mordecai was firm in his speech, yet kind. He had no desire to cause a scene; however, he was determined on this issue. No sooner had Ja'al thrown up his hands in defeat on the subject did Haman's chief guard begin bellowing his orders.

"Bow! Bow before Prime Minister Haman!" All around him Mordecai observed men hitting the dirt with their faces, as the chariot which carried Haman passed by them. Mordecai remained where he stood, as calm and as cool as ever. Haman's eyes searched the crowds from

71

his perch and locked on Mordecai. His fury there was as evident as the robe he wore.

"Dare you not bow before me, old man?" Haman spoke through his clenched teeth.

"I shall not." Mordecai inspected the apple he was holding. "I worship no man nor idol, Haman. Jehovah alone is worthy of worship," he stated looking up at the man in front of him.

"So, you are openly putting your Jewish religion before the command of the king?" Haman's eyes burned with rage.

"I have no problem bowing in respect to our king. However, if the king demands I worship you, as you require, then yes, I am." Mordecai slowly raised his apple to his mouth and took a bite.

"We'll see about this, you ignorant fool," Haman promised him. He gave the command and his chariot lurched into motion.

Mordecai watched Haman until he was out of sight. He wished he were as calm as he appeared. He could not help but feel the plan Jehovah had for both himself and Esther was about to be revealed.

Chapter 9
Subtle Persuasion and an Extreme Proposition

Haman barely picked at the meal in front of him. His appetite was lost. How could he, Haman, Prime Minister of Persia, allow one man to affect his mood to such a degree? Normally, he would not. But this man…this ONE man, was a man he had hated for years. It all made sense now. Mordecai was a Jew. A Jew! No wonder he had always hated him so! He knew there was something about him he did not like from the moment he had met him, though until now he could not put his finger on it.

"Husband, please. You must eat something," Zeresh pleaded to her husband.

"I hunger for one thing, Zeresh. The head of Mordecai on this plate!" Haman stabbed his fork through the piece of meat in front of him. "He utterly refused to bow to me. In front of others! And what did I do about it? I rode away!"

"To fight another day, Haman. Go to the king! Demand Mordecai's death! He is blatantly refusing to carry out a commandment issued directly by Ahasuerus. You know he will not allow that!"

"And he is a JEW, Zeresh!" Haman was so lost in his own thoughts, he had not heard the proposition made by his wife. "Will my family never be rid of these imbeciles!?!" Haman banged his goblet loudly on the table. "What does a man have to do to have his cup filled around here?" he demanded loudly as several servants rushed to his side, their urns filled with ale.

"As I said," Zeresh was growing impatient with Haman's irritable mood, "go to King Ahasuerus and tell him of Mordecai's treachery."

"I cannot get to the king this evening. He is in his chambers, with his queen," Haman mocked, "under strict orders not to be disturbed." Haman downed the remnants of his goblet, as he finished his statement, then threw it across the room where it crashed to the floor in a thousand pieces.

"Come, Haman! Enough of this nonsense!" Zeresh quickly rose from her place at the table and screamed in his direction. She had never spoken to her husband in such a way, but she could take no more of his whining and temper tantrums. Haman was so surprised that he could do nothing but stare at her. "Who is it that cares if one man out of an entire kingdom refuses to bow to you? I have told you to remember your place! You are the Prime Minister of Persia! Have him killed! For goodness sake, kill every Jew in the nation for all I care! Just get over your endless brooding!" Zeresh quickly stalked to a window, her face averted from Haman. She was honestly as afraid to face him as she was to have her back turned to him. He could have her killed for speaking to him in such a tone. Where had that come from?

Though Haman was in shock over the way Zeresh spoke to him, something she had said sent a sheer thrill throughout his body. Kill the Jews. All of them. He was second in command to the king. With the right proposition, he could be rid of not only Mordecai, but the entire Jewish nation. Mordecai slowly rose and crossed the room to stand behind Zeresh. He saw her tremble, anticipating a blow from him or a stern lashing at the least.

Haman lifted his hands and laid them to rest on her shoulders. "Zeresh," he spoke slowly, "that is a brilliant idea." Quickly she turned to face him.

"Haman, I am so sorry that I spoke to you in such a way. It just hurts me so to see you forlorn and in such despair." She knew she was laying it on a little thick, but she was even capable of producing a tear if it meant having her husband spare his anger.

"Zeresh, my sweet," Haman hugged her to him. "I realize you want to see our family prosper. Do not concern yourself over your words or your tone. Because of the fact that your idea was brilliant, I will let you by. This time." He finished as slowly as he began, and with a final, firm, squeeze, he let her go.

Zeresh breathed a sigh of relief. Though she believed her husband loved her, he was so consumed with hate and vengeance at the moment, she was not sure where even she stood with him. "Let us consult and devise the words I shall use. I will collect my thoughts, plan my speech and go to the king with my plea….to kill every Jew in the kingdom."

"Allow me to gather the Pur, Husband." Zeresh rushed to a drawer nearby and pulled out the ancient dice. "We shall roll the dice, and they will tell us when the execution shall take place." Zeresh handed the dice to her husband, who began to toss them gently in his hands. He was about to release them and allow them to direct his path, when Zeresh held up her hand to halt him.

"Haman, dear," she spoke as a thought formed in her lovely head, "there is one person I feel could foul our plan."

"And who exactly might that be?" her husband questioned her.

"The queen. She seems so much more tender hearted than Vashti ever was, more concerned with the well-being of those in the kingdom. I fear if she hears of the proposal before the law is declared, she may influence the king to deny your proposal."

Haman thought over that which his wife had brought to his attention and realized that she was correct in her assessment of the queen. He too had noticed how the king seemed much "softer" since his marriage to Esther. It had taken a couple of years, but now the king seemed to have lost some of his thirst for blood and had completely lost his desire for other women. She definitely had a hold of some sort on him. Yes, she could be a problem.

"Do not worry about the queen, Zeresh. I'll simply keep the king so busy with other affairs, he will not have time to visit with her until the law has been declared. Once a decree bears his signet, the king himself cannot revoke it."

Together, the couple watched as Haman dropped the dice and they stilled.

"Mark my words, Zeresh, the house of Haman will rise again," he smiled cruelly to his wife.

"Of that I have no doubt, my husband." The smile that husband and wife shared, was pure evil. If all went well with the king, every Jew in the Kingdom would be dead by the end of the year. Haman would finally have his revenge.

"What is so important, Haman, that you had me summoned, at this hour of the morning, from my private chambers where I was enjoying some time WITH MY WIFE?" That the king was displeased was a bit of an understatement.

Exactly what Haman had hoped for. He felt it would dramatize the importance of his request.

"Again, I offer my most humble apologies, Your Majesty," Haman bowed low before his king. "You know I would have never disturbed you had it not been a most urgent matter."

The king took a deep breath and calmed himself. True, Haman had never disturbed him in this manner before, and besides himself and the queen, the king fully trusted no one in the palace, other than Haman.

"Fine, you have my audience and my attention Haman. What is it that you need?" The king settled himself and cleared his mind to give Haman his full attention. "I am listening," he confirmed.

"Your Majesty, it has sadly come to my attention that there is a certain group of ...people, for lack of a better word, scattered about your empire, who choose to follow their own set of laws instead of those which are set in place by you yourself. They choose to ignore your laws, My King, and in turn create their own set of commandments, which they follow religiously. They offer nothing to our society, nor to the land. In fact, they merely consume goods and take up space that could be used by the good people of your kingdom. By YOUR followers. I feel this treason must not continue a moment more! I had to inform you immediately!" Haman added for emphasis. He could tell he had successfully captured the king's attention by the look of contemplation which crossed his face.

"And you know this for certainty, Haman?" the king asked curiously.

"Yes, Your Majesty. I have witnessed certain of their people blatantly breaking your laws myself."

"Do you have a suggestion as to a solution to this problem?"

"Actually, Your Grace, I have. I believe it is in the best interest of the kingdom, to dispose of the entire race of these people. After all, your subjects are currently loyal and more than willing to abide by your laws. We do not need them to witness others in their presence doing otherwise and getting by with it. I believe the best solution to the problem is to make an example of the offenders by public execution."

The look on the king's face troubled Haman. What was happening to his king? There was a time he would have charged out of the palace, sword in hand himself, ready to slay anyone who defied him. This queen was ruining him! Haman continued quickly before the king had a chance to deny his request.

"I do realize, Your Majesty, that a task of such magnitude will result in a loss of income to the palace due to the fact that these people are currently tax paying citizens. Therefore, if you see fit to write this act into law, I myself shall cover the cost of the task as well as the cost of any losses our kingdom experiences because of it."

"You are willing to part with your own currency, Haman? That could be quite a sum."

"Approximately ten thousand talents of silver, My Lord," he spoke slowly, "yet such a small amount to protect our vast empire." Haman looked to the floor as if the thought of failure to be an asset to his king was more than he could bear.

"Very well, Haman." What happened next was even hard for Haman to comprehend. It was more perfect than he had ever imagined. Without another thought or another word, the king removed his ring from his hand and handed it to Haman.

"My Lord?" Haman questioned him.

"Take my signet ring, Haman. Whatever law you feel should be in place, write it. This ring will provide my name. Nothing else is needed to execute the ruling. You have come before me with a valid requisition in the best interest of my kingdom. You will do with these people as you see fit and the palace will cover the cost."

Haman took the ring from the king and quickly squelched his desire to jump up and down, clicking his heels. "My Lord," he bowed low, "the honor you have bestowed upon me leaves me without words."

"You have served me well, Haman. Rise and carry through with your plan." The king began to walk away. "I am most eager to return to my wife." Though Haman had all he needed, he still felt nervous about the king returning to the queen so quickly after he had been granted permission to carry out such a ruling. It took time to assemble the scribes and seal the document which would be the law. In that time, he was afraid the queen may learn of his request and protest. Before the decree was sealed, the king would still be able to withdrawal his approval.

"Your Majesty," Haman began. King Ahasuerus turned to face his Prime Minister. "I must say again, how honored I am that you have entrusted me with such a task; however, I would feel better were you to offer your guidance on the undertaking of such a ruling."

The king took a deep breath and turned on his heels to return to the seat he had so quickly vacated.

"Very well, Haman," he said as he returned. "Let us discuss the minor details. I am sure the queen will forgive me a few moments more."

"Allow me to go ahead and call for the scribes, Your Majesty." With a wave of the king's hand, it was done.

Chapter 10
A Time of Mourning

Esther worked patiently on the tapestry before her. Na'ila and Judith had gone into the village and only Sophia remained with the queen. Their conversation was light and had ventured onto talk of the courtship taking place between Sophia and Sayyid.

"I cannot imagine one more well-suited for you, Sophia," the queen was saying. "Sayyid cannot keep his eyes from you when you are in the same room together, and when Jamal was assisting you from the chariot last week, I thought Sayyid's head would burst as Jamal took your hand!"

Sophia threw her beautiful head back in a fit of laughter. "He is so jealous!" she laughed. As her laughter dissolved, she added on a more serious note, "However, I do not know how to handle our courtship at times. There are occasions when we are enjoying a walk in the courtyard or in the gardens that it seems he cannot bear to allow me to leave his side. Yet at other times, he seems so distant from me."

"I am afraid advice on courtship is not something I can easily give," the queen answered her honestly. "The king and I did not share a long engagement." Sophia sensed a tone of sadness in her voice as she spoke of the king.

"But you are happy within your marriage, are you not, My Queen?" Sophia hoped she had not asked a question which seemed too bold, but her relationship with Queen Esther ran much deeper than the others. They were, in fact, extremely close friends.

Esther pondered the question; she wanted to answer honestly. Dare she share with her lady-in-waiting the deep secret she had hidden for years? She had yet to speak of her heritage to anyone, including her husband. The secret, at times, weighed heavily on her heart, and there were days, as those in the recent past, that it bothered her more than others to be keeping something so important from those she held dear. She could not explain it, but she felt sharing her secret with her husband and those around her was something she would eventually do. However, that was not where the current conversation had led. She continued to follow the directions of Mordecai and keep her secret. Esther opted to stick to the facts.

"Oh, yes, Sophia, I am very happy. Just lonely at times I suppose. When we were first married, there were very few nights I spent away from the king. As time passed, those scarce nights turned out to be more frequent, yet still no more than a week or two would pass before he would call for me. Now, I feel I am losing some of my appeal to my king, for it has been a long while since he has sought me."

Sophia could not miss the tear which silently dropped from the queen's cheek onto her tapestry. Immediately she was at her feet, embracing the queen's hands with her own.

"Your Highness, I am so sorry to have brought despair to your heart with my thoughtless questions. Of course, His Majesty is busy with matters of the kingdom and has not been able to pull himself away. It bears no reflection on his love for you."

Esther stood quickly and wiped the tears from her cheek. "Of course not, Sophia. I am sorry to have burdened you with my mindless chatter. He will send for me when time allows."

"Is it terribly improper for you to initiate a meeting yourself, My Queen?" Sophia asked, hoping she would not again cause tears to fall from her beloved queen's face. She knew commoners were not welcome in the king's presence without being summoned, but perhaps his queen was different.

"I cannot, Sophia! Even I am not allowed in the presence of King Ahasuerus unless he sends for me. To attempt such a visit is a death sentence. If someone approaches the king, and he extends his golden scepter, they are allowed to approach and all is well. However, if he does not extend his golden scepter allowing them to come forward, they are immediately removed from his presence and put to death. That includes me as well." Esther had approached a looking glass and stood gazing at her own reflection. She saw Sophia come up behind her and watched as her friend rested her hands on her shoulders.

"Do you know what this reminds me of, My Queen?" Esther watched her friend in the glass. "It reminds of a night, several years ago, just like this. On that night, we looked together into this same looking glass and I assured you then, as I am assuring you now, that the king would have but one look at you and his heart would be lost to all others. He has merely forgotten the beauty which has been kept hidden in these chambers. Once his business slows, and he thinks again of your lovely face and the sweet spirit, which he now knows indwells you, he will fall in love with you all over again and will not be able to withhold himself from you a moment longer. You have taught me to have faith, My Queen. You have taught me of your Jehovah and have assured me that He knows all that transpires. He knows of this too, Your Majesty. Do not let go of that faith you have so often taught me about."

Esther turned into her friend's sweet embrace. How precious this woman was to her. "Sophia, I could not make it in this place without you. Jehovah has blessed me beyond measure with not only your companionship but with your friendship as well." Esther broke the embrace and again wiped the tears from her face just as the door to her chambers opened. Na'ila approached, without permission, and the look on her face caused fear to course through Esther at an alarming speed.

"Na'ila! Whatever is wrong?" It was Sophia's voice who cut through the quiet. "Where is Judith?" she continued to question when she realized Na'ila had come in alone.

"My Queen," Na'ila began, "your dear friend, Mordecai, sits outside the king's gate. He is clothed in sackcloth and pours ashes upon his head."

Confusion was evident on the queen's face. "Clothes of mourning?" Esther questioned her. "Whatever for? Why would Mordecai sit outside the king's gate in clothes of mourning?" Esther looked to Sophia who shook her head in reply. "Na'ila," Esther continued, "quickly gather appropriate raiment and take them straight to Mordecai. Take the sackcloth from him so that he may enter into the gate once again."

"Yes, My Queen." Na'ila quickly bowed and left the room to do as the queen commanded her.

Turning back to Sophia, Esther again voiced the question they both were thinking. "Why is Mordecai in mourning?"

"I do not know, Your Majesty. Where was Judith?" Sophia questioned in return.

"Perhaps when Na'ila returns, she can answer both our questions. Once Mordecai is again properly clothed and inside the king's gate, I wish to go to him and see what this is all about."

"Yes, My Queen." Sophia agreed.

Not many moments passed before Na'ila was again at the door to the queen's chambers. She did not come empty handed, but the garments she handed to the queen caused a knot in her stomach. "He refused them, Your Majesty," Na'ila apologized. "I fear there is more to his disposition than poor attire."

The alarm that went through Esther was enough to cause her knees to tremble. That something was very wrong was obvious. The question was, what? Esther needed answers. Now.

"Sophia, summon Hatach immediately." Sophia all but ran from the room. Esther was speaking of one of the king's chamberlains whom he appointed to assist her when needed. Esther paced the confines of her room. Her stomach ached, her head hurt, and her legs felt as if they would give way at any moment. A feeling of dread was sweeping through her entire body, but now was not the time for rash actions or for a rampant imagination.

Hatach was in her presence within a matter of minutes and Esther quickly made her request known. He was to go to Mordecai outside the king's gate, find out what was wrong and return to her with the answer within the hour. Na'ila remained along with Sophia by the queen's side. It was during this quiet moment that Sophia realized Judith had still not returned.

"Na'ila," Sophia questioned, "what has become of Judith?"

"I know not," Na'ila answered honestly. "She was with me until we saw Mordecai. I ran straight to the queen's chambers to inform her of his state, thinking Judith was behind me, yet when I entered, I was alone."

At that moment there was a knock at the queen's door. "Enter," she commanded.

Hatach entered the room, Judith behind him.

"Your Majesty," Hatach bowed. "I fear the news I bring will cause you extreme grief. Should we speak alone?"

"Your Majesty, I already know of that which Hatach speaks," Judith spoke up. "When Na'ila ran ahead to inform you of Mordecai's state, I hid myself near to him to see if I could find out why he was mourning. I am embarrassed to say I was standing near as he revealed his reason for despair to Hatach."

Esther was not sure, but she felt as if some very pertinent information regarding her heritage would be revealed very soon. "Hatach, you may speak freely. I have complete confidence in these ladies of my court."

"As you wish, My Queen," he began. "Upon speaking with Mordecai I have learned some treacherous news as far as the Jews of our provinces are concerned. The king has written into law, that every Jew—man, woman and child—shall be executed before the end of the year. Your dear friend, Mordecai, has proclaimed to Prime Minister Haman that he is indeed a Jew."

Esther's hand immediately went to her heart. "Mordecai must have misunderstood, Hatach! Surely the king could not be so cruel! The Jews are among the king's most loyal subjects! "

"As proof, Your Majesty, Mordecai was able to provide me with the written decree." Esther took the parchment from his hand which he held out to her. Hatach did not miss the way her hands trembled.

Upon reading the decree, Esther sank to the floor.

"Your Majesty!" Sophia cried as she rushed to her queen's side.

"It says here," Esther tried to continue, "that on the thirteenth day of the month Adar, of this very year, it is decreed that every Jew—man, woman and child—shall be killed by any who shall come upon them. It also states that the possessions of those who are killed will become property of those who take their lives." A sob broke Esther's voice as she dropped the parchment to the floor.

Judith reached down to retrieve the decree and slowly finished what Esther could not. "This order shall be carried out in the name of King Ahasuerus."

"There is more, Your Majesty," Hatach continued carefully.

Esther attempted to clear the spinning of her head to pay attention to the chamberlain's words. "Mordecai has made a request of you. He asks that you go to the king and plead for the lives of his people."

Esther's heart broke at those words. Those in her company had no idea that the lives she was asked to plead for were not only the life of the dear cousin who had raised her, but the lives of her very own people. Esther calmed her racing heart and stood to face Hatach.

"Hatach, return to Mordecai. Let him know that I am not at liberty to seek out the king." Esther did not stop the tears that streaked her face. "Please tell him, I have not been summoned by the king in thirty days. Law will not allow me to enter his presence apart from his summons. I would most certainly face certain death were I to go against this commandment and seek him out on my own."

"Your Majesty." Hatach bowed to her and then he was gone. It physically hurt him to see his queen so distraught. Esther did not feel she could stand a moment longer. Making her way into her private chambers, she fell upon her bed and openly wept.

Chapter 11
A Time Such as This

Esther remained in her private chambers much longer than she had meant to. She had cried herself into a brief fitful sleep, and when she awoke, the sun was beginning to dip below the palace walls. She knew her court would be upset after her departure, and she wanted to calm their nerves. However, she must first completely calm her own.

As she rose, a thought that she could not believe had taken so long to cross her mind occurred to her. Mordecai had taught her that Jehovah was in control of every situation. Nothing was impossible for Him. With that thought, Esther sank to her knees beside her bed.

Tears, again, began to fall, but these tears were different. Instead of tears of panic and fear, these tears were tears of pleading to her God. The God she knew had led her to this place. The God she knew controlled every situation. The God she knew would lead her through this. She prayed for a calm disposition. She prayed for wisdom in handling the situation. She prayed for Mordecai and others across the nation who were in a state of constant mourning.

As she concluded her prayer and rose from her knees, a knock sounded on her door. She opened it to find Sophia on the outside, her own beautiful face stained with tears.

"My Queen, I am sorry to disturb you, but Hatach brings more news from Mordecai and has asked to speak to you concerning this."

Esther walked slowly into the open chamber to find Hatach, Na'ila, and Judith standing in anticipation of her arrival. They each bowed upon seeing her, but she could tell their hearts were heavy. They loved her and they hurt for her. However, only one of them knew the full extent of the reason for her grief.

"Yes, Hatach. You have more news from Mordecai?"

Hatach raised his head, but kept his eyes downcast. He could not bear to look into her face, as he now realized the death sentence he had delivered included this woman he so admired. "Your Majesty," Hatach took a deep breath before he could continue and then did so slowly, "Mordecai asked me to relay the message to you, that although you are indeed the Queen of Persia, the decree openly declares that **ALL** the Jews be killed on the thirteenth day of the month of Adar. Both young and old, little children, and women. No Jew will be spared—including you, My Queen."

The gasp that was heard throughout the room was numbing. Esther closed her eyes to steady herself. Of course the decree included her. No one in the palace until this moment knew of Esther's heritage. However, it would be found out and she would not be spared. Once the decree was signed, the king himself could not reverse it.

It was suddenly very clear to Esther as to her purpose here. It was not coincidence that she had found favor with the king and had been chosen as his queen. It was not coincidence that, until recently, he seemed to have true, affectionate feelings for her beyond simply a physical attraction to her. None of the events which had taken place in her life had been coincidence. They had all been God.

"Hatach, I do not wish, the information you have shared to leave this room. Is that understood?" She looked to the king's chamberlain and to each of the ladies of her court. They each bowed their heads and conveyed their promise of confidentiality.

"Your Majesty," Hatach continued quickly, "Mordecai did add that if you continue to hold onto your secret at this time, the Jews will be delivered in another time, from another place. He said Jehovah has promised to preserve the Jews. However, you, as well as your family, will be destroyed during this slaughter. He said perhaps you have come to the kingdom for such a time as this. Perhaps you may be able to stop the massacre before it begins."

Esther was afraid, but she knew her path was set before her. She knew what she had to do.

"Return to Mordecai once more, Hatach. Tell him, I will go unto the king, although law prohibits it. I will do what I can to try to save my people." Esther was confident in her decision. She did not know how this all would end, but she did know what she would do, and the peace she was currently experiencing was purely heaven sent.

"Your Majesty!" Sophia begged of her. "Please reconsider! Remember what you told me just earlier today. If you go unto the king, and he does not wish to see you, you will face certain death!"

Esther looked to her companion and dearest friend. She then turned back to the king's chamberlain with a complete answer for Mordecai. "Hatach, tell Mordecai to gather all the Jews who are present in Shushan. Have them fast for me, eating or drinking nothing for three days and three nights. My maidens and I will do the same. At the end of three days and three nights, I will go unto the king, and if I perish, I perish," she finished confidently.

"Yes, My Queen. As you wish." Hatach turned to walk away but stopped and turned to look at his queen once more. "Your Majesty," he spoke and she noticed his voice seemed weak.

"Yes, Hatach?" she asked.

"I am not a Jew, but I will do all in my power to assist you with this quest. I too shall fast, and perhaps one day you can explain to me the reason why." With that, he bowed once more, then turned and walked away.

Chapter 12
A Feast Fit for a King

Three days passed by quickly for Esther. She and her maidens fasted as promised. Mordecai had assembled all the Jews in Shushan together and they too fasted as promised. Hatach fasted, and Sophia had been granted permission to tell Sayyid of all that was happening, and he too joined the fast.

Esther had many friends as well as family aiding her in prayer and supplication to Jehovah. She was not alone in her endeavor. She had been afraid that once her Jewish heritage was discovered by those closest to her, their allegiance might change, but it was evident that God had been at work in their hearts as well. Instead of rebuking their queen, they embraced her cause, as well as her religious views, and aided her in her quest. If her cause before the king went unheeded and she was not successful in saving her Jewish people, at least she had been given the opportunity to share her God with these dear friends. The three days before she went unto the king had not been wasted.

Also, Esther had pondered the insane ruling and questioned the reason behind it. Ahasuerus had never mentioned a problem with the Jews before. He had also changed immensely since their marriage. She was certain he was much less of the blood-thirsty king he had been in former days. She had heard of the savage warrior he had been in the past, but he had shown none of that behavior since their time together. Their marriage was far from perfect, especially in the course of the last month, but until this time, she had been happy as his queen.

Suddenly, Haman came to her mind. She could not help but feel that he was somehow behind all that had transpired. Since Ahasuerus had promoted him to prime minister, Haman had carried an ego the size of the palace with him everywhere he went. Esther thought back over the past months. She had witnessed how Haman walked through the streets during the busiest parts of the day, just to gloat as the people bowed to him. And, she had heard how Mordecai refused to bow, proclaiming his worship solely for the Jehovah they served. Yes, Esther realized, it must be Haman's influence behind the terrible ruling to eradicate her people.

It was now the appointed day. Esther arose early and spent extra time in prayer. Then she and her maidens spent hours readying her for her approach to the king. She bathed in perfumed oils. Her hair was brushed until it shone, then pulled away from her face and braided into a bun at the base of her neck. Small trundles were left hanging around her face. At last, she stepped into her royal apparel, the soft blue cape falling from her shoulders in waves where it reached the floor. The final touch, the queen jewels, which she had acquired on the day she had been crowned, were draped around her neck. The crown in place atop her head made her look exactly like the queen she was. With a final hug for each of the ladies in her court, Esther bid them farewell, forbidding the tears they tried not to shed.

"Have faith that I will return, and when I do, be ready as we have planned," she commanded them.

She could not explain how she felt as she approached the inner court of the king. She was scared, knowing not if she would live or die. Yet, whichever way the ruling went, if she was accepted or denied, she knew that Jehovah was in control and nothing would happen which He did not allow.

Esther rounded the final corner that led to the inner court. She saw the look which crossed Jamal's face as she neared him and then stopped in front of him. It was a look of shock and then of fear. Fear for her own safety.

"I wish an audience with King Ahasuerus," she spoke softly and calmly. Jamal swallowed hard and his breathing seemed labored although he stood completely still. He spoke in a hushed tone so as not to gain the attention of the king who was visibly seated on his throne in the adjoining room.

"My Queen, please, the king has not yet seen you. Please reconsider your request while there is still time. You know what will happen if his scepter is not extended to you." He saw the determined look in his queen's eyes and knew his plea was falling on deaf ears. "Please, My Lady. I beg of you. Do not make this mistake!"

Her heart was pounding, yet she would not turn back and flee as she was so urged to do. "I thank you for your concern, Jamal, however, if it is indeed a mistake, it is mine to make." Esther took a breath to calm her nerves, then a bit louder proclaimed, "I wish to see King Ahasuerus."

Jamal closed his eyes in defeat as he heard the king arise from his place on the throne. "Queen Esther? Is that your voice I hear?" he called from the throne room.

Esther stepped around Jamal who was silently begging her to run from the kingdom as fast as she could.

"It is I, My King." Esther smiled her brightest smile in his direction. Slowly Jamal turned to see if he would be allowed to grant her passage to His Majesty or if he would be forced to drag her away to her death. Relief was evident to each of them as the king slowly extended his golden scepter in her direction.

Esther entered the inner court and walked toward his throne. He had forgotten just how beautiful she was. Her smile did so much for his heavy heart. How had he let so much time pass since their last meeting?

"My Queen," he welcomed her as she approached and reached to touch the end of the golden scepter. "For what reason do I owe the pleasure of your presence before me? What is it that you require? You shall have whatever you desire, up to half of the kingdom."

"Your Majesty," she bowed before him and rose with a smile he could not possibly refuse. "If it is agreeable with you, and if I have gained favor in your sight, I wish for you and Haman to join me this day in my chambers at a banquet I have prepared for you."

"A banquet? You have prepared a banquet for me?" the king questioned her. He was clearly shocked that she had not requested something more for herself.

"Yes, My King. I have missed your company and have prepared a banquet for you, myself, and Prime Minister Haman to enjoy." Esther kept the smile on her face, though her fear of being rejected was mounting. Her fear was short lived.

"Cause Haman to make haste!" he called to a servant nearby. "We have a feast to attend!" The king reached for her hand and gently kissed the back of it as she offered it to him. "Your beauty is simply breathtaking, My Queen."

"Thank you, Your Majesty," Esther bowed her head to him shyly. "I will see you within the hour then?" Her joy at his acceptance was obvious.

"You shall," he affirmed.

"Wonderful. If you will excuse me then. I will return to make sure everything is ready for your arrival. My King." Esther bowed once again and slowly turned to walk away. She glanced back over her shoulder to find him still gazing at her as she rounded the corner of the inner chamber and cast him one last smile.

Jamal stood at attention as she exited, and once she had cleared the presence of any and all who could see her, she exhaled the breath she had been holding and fell momentarily to her knees. Right in the middle of the palace hallway, she allowed her tears to fall as she took a moment to thank Jehovah for His precious intervention. She knew her life was spared simply because He had willed it so. She prayed for continued guidance to follow His lead and not rush into the reason for her actions, though she wanted to immediately plead for the king's mercies on her people. She quickly returned to her feet and rushed to her chambers to make sure all was ready for the arrival of the king and Haman.

Her maidens were ecstatic once she had arrived back to her quarters. Once brief hugs were exchanged and tears of joy wiped from their faces, Esther hurried into the dining chamber to make sure all was prepared and ready.

The table was set with the finest dining and serving pieces available. Clusters of grapes served as decoration as well as an addition to the full meal. Esther was confident the king would be pleased with the spread before him.

Before she realized it, the king and Haman had arrived, feasted to their fill, and were about to return to their own quarters. She had not missed how Haman acted as if he himself were the host of the entire affair.

"My Queen," the king began before their departure, "what is thy petition? Name your request, up to half the kingdom, and it shall be given thee."

Esther looked deep into the eyes of her king. She listened for the advice of Jehovah. A moment passed before she begin to slowly speak. "My petition and request is this, O King. If I have found favor in thy sight and if you agree to my petition…" Esther paused a moment and then continued, her eyes never leaving his. She noticed how he was hanging on her every word and took that as a good sign. "…please come again to my chambers tomorrow. Bring Haman once more to a banquet I shall prepare for you, and I will name my request as you ask."

The king could not break the gaze she had instituted, nor her heart by refusing her. He had missed his queen. "It shall be so," he promised her. "Until tomorrow then." Once Esther made her request known, she shyly lowered her gaze. The king adored her innocence and stood to leave reluctantly, followed by Haman.

"My Queen," the Prime Minister began. He reached for her hand and she quickly turned away from him to follow the king to her door. That she was ignoring him was plainly obvious to Haman, but unnoticed by the king. "My Queen," he tried again.

"Yes, Prime Minister Haman?" she asked nonchalantly from the other side of the room.

"Thank you for your hospitality this evening," he bowed to her.

Esther smiled in his direction, though her attention was on the king.

"Of course, Haman. Until tomorrow." Esther stood by the door as the king once again took and kissed the back of her hand.

"My Queen," he dipped his head in her direction as he and Haman exited her chambers—Esther noticing that Haman exited first.

Chapter 13
All but One

Haman headed out that afternoon with a spring in his step and a glimmer in his eye. He had been invited to a banquet with the queen. And not just the banquet today but another tomorrow! How proud he was of himself for obtaining her favor. Clearly, he had been mistaken earlier. She simply had not heard him call to her the first time. After all, she herself had specifically requested his presence at each of her affairs.

Haman still loved the way the people bowed as he passed. He would never tire of that. In just a few short months he had obtained the king's signet ring which allowed him to write and implement any law he saw fit. He would very soon be rid of the Jews whom he so hated, without it costing him one cent, and best of all, his vengeance on Mordecai would be complete. Revenge was his for the taking! How he loved being himself! Life could not get much better for

Haman. Nothing could sour his mood this day…except what happened next.

Haman approached the king's gate where many were gathered and joined in various conversations. As they saw Haman approach, they each hit their faces in the dirt in an effort to bow before he passed. All but one.

Mordecai sat directly in Haman's path, laughing with his companions and enjoying a large, juicy apple. As his companions fell to their faces, Mordecai remained in his current position. Watching as Haman approached, he did not move, except to lift his apple to his mouth and enjoy a bite. Surely this ignorant fool would not again try to evoke the wrath of the mighty Haman!

Haman stopped in front of him and waited as Mordecai began to move from his seat to allow him passage. At last. Seeing Mordecai bow before him would be the finale to his absolutely perfect day! He would have to refrain from placing his perfect foot on the back of the head of Mordecai and grinding his face into the dirt, but he did not want to dirty his soles.

Haman stood proud and tall, anxious to watch Mordecai rise and bow. But to his utter surprise, Mordecai's action was not for the intention of rising at all. In actuality, his body never left the chair from which he was seated! He was simply shifting his weight, making himself more comfortable! Haman watched as Mordecai continued to enjoy the apple he was slowly consuming. Their eyes met in an icy glare and Haman knew, once again, that he had lost another round to Mordecai. Mordecai had no intention of bowing. He had no intention of MOVING!

Haman began to ease his way around Mordecai. Mordecai watching him pass, moving not a muscle save from the hand which was holding his apple. It took everything within Haman's power not to reach out and strike him where he sat, forcing him to bow as he picked himself up from the dirt! He chose to refrain, for now.

As Haman stalked away, Mordecai knew the fire he had kindled in Haman was at full blast.

"Why do you provoke him, Mordecai?" one of his companions asked as he rose from his bowed position. "You already know the Jews are to be slaughtered, no doubt beginning with you and your family. Perhaps if you bow to him now, Haman would forgive your sin and spare your life, along with the other Jews."

"I have told you," Mordecai spoke as he continued to watch Haman walk away, "I worship none but the one, true God. My sins are not for Haman to forgive, but God and God alone. I have begged Jehovah's forgiveness for many aspects and wrongdoings within my life, however, worshipping man will not be a sin I will have to plead forgiveness for. Haman deserves neither worship nor my respect."

Haman stormed through the doors of his home, yelling for Zeresh before his foot had crossed the threshold.

"Zeresh! Gather Memucan, Tarshish, Shethar and Meres! I wish to speak with you all!" Haman slouched onto his couch and demanded wine and grapes from the servants. Mordecai had ruined his perfect day, but he would get by with it! "And bring them NOW!" he bellowed.

Zeresh quickly sent her servants into the streets and into their homes to gather the friends Haman had instructed. Within the hour, she had produced them all and they were seated in the main room of the house.

"What is so urgent that you have summoned us all to come unto your home at this hour, Haman?" Each of the men, along with Zeresh, were comfortably seated with goblets full of wine awaiting Haman to speak his mind.

"Look around you," he began. "There is nothing of want which I do not possess. I, myself, am comely to look at. I have a beautiful wife. She has borne me ten fine strapping sons. I am second-in-command to the King of Persia. I have been placed in a position higher than each of you, as I bear his signet ring! I have the authority to write and implement any law I see fit!" Haman slammed his fist into the table. "I was summoned to a banquet today, by the queen, with none other than herself, I, and the king in attendance!" Haman stood and paced the room.

"AND, I am invited to another with only herself and the king tomorrow!"

Zeresh watched her husband and the faces of the friends she had gathered at his command. So what if they looked a bit put out by her husband's proclamations. He had accomplished much, and she was proud of him. Her husband's house had risen again, which included herself. She enjoyed the finer things of life, and after all, that is what really mattered to her. Yes, he was being a little arrogant, but he deserved it. He was speaking the truth in all that he said. They were, after all, privileged that he had called for them by name and that they were being allowed to sit with them and share in their finest wine.

"However," Haman continued as he paced, "all of my riches, all of my glory, all of the honor due me and the fame I possess, none of it means anything to me as long as I see Mordecai the Jew sitting at the king's gate!" He was yelling now, although speaking through clenched teeth, and again, his goblet left his hand in a fierce throw.

Zeresh watched it crash and the contents stream down the wall. This happened so often now that she barely even flinched.

"Hang him," she spoke out.

"What?" Haman looked at his wife as if she had lost her senses.

"Hang him," she repeated matter-of-factly. "Better yet, hang him in such a way that none other will ever again question the commands of Prime Minister Haman." Zeresh smiled an evil smile, then rolled her eyes and sighed as all others in her company continued to stare blankly in her direction.

"Haman, you have plenty of servants, and four others here in our present company. Build a gallows, seventy-five feet tall, right outside our gate. None will be able to miss it. Tomorrow, rise, go directly to the king, tell him of Mordecai's repeated treachery and hang him. Everyone will see that to rebuke Prime Minister Haman results in sudden death. Once that's done, you will feel much more at peace and be able to enjoy the banquet set before you by the queen."

As if they were discussing nothing more than the subject of the weather, Zeresh rose and left the room, Haman watching her walk away.

A smile split his face as he looked to the others in attendance. "I like it," he grinned. Within the hour, hammers begin piercing the dark night right outside Haman's home. Haman, however, was not about to waste his time building the gallows; he had men to see to that. He was headed to the outward court to see to more important things. First thing in the morning, as the king awoke and began his day after his restful night's sleep, Haman would be present to petition him. Mordecai would be dead by noon.

Chapter 14
Divine Intervention

King Ahasuerus tossed and turned, his sheets tangled about him. In all his years, he had never had trouble sleeping. Nor, in all his years, had he ever had a woman to encompass his mind as this one had. How had he allowed his business affairs to interrupt what he was so obviously achieving in his relationship with Queen Esther? Especially, right after he had declared to her that he would not allow it to do so. The King smothered his face with his pillow once again.

Never had he seen a woman so beautiful. Not only was he extremely physically attracted to her, but he was also attracted to the sweet innocence and kind spirit she possessed as well. She was truly a wise choice as his queen. He would love to send for her immediately, and he had no doubt she would be obediently in his arms in but a moment; however, something kept him from doing so.

He was extremely embarrassed to call for her now after so much time had gone by since he had initiated their last meeting. He had expected her to be cross with him after only a couple weeks, of time had passed, and that had kept him from doing so before, but today she had risked her own life and sought him out herself in an effort to spend time with him. Yet she did not grieve him about his absence, but asked for permission to deliver unto him a feast in his honor. He now knew she was not cross and that alone added to his respect of her.

Another cause for his hesitation was due to that respect for her; he did not wish to inconvenience her at such an hour, as she was sure to be settled in her own chambers by now. "What is wrong with me," the king wondered aloud. "Never before have I cared whom I inconvenience. I never once thought of the time when I would send for Vashti. I called for her at any and all hours of the night or day, never wondering if it was of convenience to her. Perhaps that is why our marriage ended as it did. I did not allow enough thought of her feelings or comfort, much less whether or not it was convenient for her. "

He turned over onto his side in another effort to comfort himself. This too proved uncomfortable to the king which led to another thought. *I've never concerned myself with the comfort of the maids in the Court of the Women either. I've never given thought to how they feel at being summoned as I desire. Of course, I have not sent for any of them since I married Esther. But why haven't I? Just because I know the realization of such would prove unfaithful and uncomfortable to my current queen? I am the King of Persia! My comfort and convenience should come before everyone else's. Shouldn't it?* He flopped onto his back again.

But Esther. Oh, Esther is so different. The king realized a grin had split his face in the darkness of his room. Quickly he schooled his features although no one could see him. *Perhaps I have not sent for her because I am afraid of this, this pounding of my heart whenever she is near. Just the thought of her puts my head in a spin. Those eyes. That smile. Oh, that smile. But, how can I rule my empire efficiently and effectively when my queen is such a distraction to me?*

The king closed his eyes and thought of Esther. He could not be sure, but he was quite certain that this he felt for her, this feeling that filled every part of him, was indeed caused by the little four-letter word he was so often warned about—the word which had the power to turn noble kings into flighty peasant boys. The word which could cause a ruler to make decisions with his heart in place of his head. The word which could cause an empire to fall if not governed properly. Love.

Yes, he feared he was in love with his queen. But was that all bad? He immensely enjoyed his time with her. She seemed to alleviate the stresses of the kingdom with her gentle touch and kind words. This would help him rule more compassionately and make wiser decisions for his people, would it not? Could he not love his queen and be a fine, powerful king at the same time? Ah, the mysteries of the heart.

Speaking of mysteries, he loved the mysterious way Esther eluded him. Again, he thought aloud in the empty room. "What could it be that she desires so desperately that it requires a second feast?" He did not think she required items of material value or surely she would have voiced that today. The king punched at his pillow in agitation. Just another thought to consume his mind when he should be sleeping. He had to be at his best tomorrow when he again feasted with his queen. He had to get some sleep!

"My Lord," he heard a knock on the door. He did not rise from his bed but slapped his hand to his forehead.

"Enter!" he demanded, albeit a bit gruffly.

"Sire, please excuse my intrusion; I knew you to be alone in your chambers, but I thought I heard voices and wanted to assure myself of your safety."

"Yes, thank you, Ja'al. I am quite well, and quite alone, although sleepless at the moment."

"Your Majesty, is there something I can get for you?" Ja'al questioned. He was a bit concerned. He had never known a night his king could not sleep, though he had been the chief chamberlain to guard his door since the incident with Bigthan and Teresh several years before.

"Actually, yes, there is." The king sat up in bed and gave specific instructions to his chamberlain. "Ja'al send for the book of Chronicles and someone to read them to me. Perhaps that could lure me to sleep."

"As you wish, Your Majesty." Ja'al bowed his way out the door and within a few moments, the king was joined in his chambers by a servant reading the Chronicles of the Kings.

Hoping for boredom to bring on sleep, the king listened to the servant begin the reading of the histories and genealogy of the kings before him. Sleep was slow, but it was coming, until something the servant read caught his attention.

"Stop!" the king commanded as he sat straight up in his bed once again. "Read that again, the last section you just read."

The servant retraced his reading and began again. *In those days, while Mordecai sat in the king's gate, two of the king's chamberlains, Bigthan and Teresh, of those which kept the door, were wroth, and sought to lay hand on the King Ahasuerus.*"

"Continue!" the king commanded him when the servant stopped to look his direction.

"And the thing was known to Mordecai, who told it unto Esther the queen; and Esther certified the king thereof in Mordecai's name. And when inquisition was made of the matter, it was found out; therefore they were both hanged on a tree."

"Your Majesty," the servant inquired, "shall I continue?"

"What was done for Mordecai for this?" the king asked.

"I believe nothing, Sire. Nothing that anyone is aware of in any way," the servant admitted.

King Ahasuerus sprang from his bed, grabbing his robe as he rose. "Who is in the court? I cannot believe I have allowed this to go unnoticed!" The king paced in front of his bed. "Who is in the court? Someone must be out there!" he wanted answers and he wanted them now.

"Haman, my Lord. Prime Minister Haman was coming into the outer court as I was coming to read for you," the servant answered quickly.

"Send him in! I wish to see him. NOW!" the king demanded.

The servant hurried from his place, almost forgetting in his haste to bow as he left to fetch Haman for the king. The king paced the confines of his room, impatiently awaiting Haman's arrival. At last his second-in-command entered his chambers.

"You requested my presence, My King?" Haman bowed, his chest puffed with pride that he had been summoned.

"Haman. What should I do for the man whom I delight to honor?" the king stopped pacing and stood directly in front of Haman.

Haman's heart skipped a beat. He almost told the king he had all the honor due him, as he was already second-in-command, bore the king's own signet ring, and could prepare any decrees he saw fit, but he decided he might as well use the opportunity to take whatever it was the king was willing to give him. Haman pondered the thought for a moment. What do I desire from the king, he thought? More of the same, yet on an even grander scale, of course.

Haman smiled as he delivered his ideas to the king. His idea was phenomenal. "My King, let the royal apparel be brought which the king use to wear, and the horse that the King rideth upon, and the crown royal which is set upon his head, and let this apparel and horse be delivered by one of the king's most noble princes, that they may array the man whom you delight to honor, and parade him through the streets of the city, and proclaim before him. Thus shall it be done to the man whom the king delights to honor!" Haman could not wait for his parade! How he loved his perfect life!

Ahasuerus thought for a moment. "Perfect!" he proclaimed! "Make haste, Haman! Take the apparel and the horse, as thou hast said, and do even so to Mordecai the Jew, that sitteth at the king's gate."

Haman felt as if the wind had been knocked out of him. "My King?" he questioned.

"Let nothing fail of all that which thou has spoken! Make haste Haman! I wish for Mordecai to be honored immediately! And Haman," he finished, "make sure you are the one to lead him through the streets! You are, after all, my second-in-command."

"Yes, Your Majesty. As you wish." Haman tried very hard to breathe but was having a very hard time controlling his emotions. He himself, was about to honor the man whom he hated beyond all measure—the same man whom he was about to request from the king permission to hang immediately. The man whom he had written a law to kill. And not only him but every one of his heritage. Mordecai was about to be led through the streets, wearing the king's garments, wearing the king's crown, on the king's horse, being led by the very man who sought to destroy him! Where had this gone so drastically wrong?

"Haman?" the king's voice brought him back to the here and now.

"Yes...yes, Your Majesty?" Haman spoke, bringing his thoughts back to the present time.

"Why are you still here? Go!" the king commanded as he motioned for Haman to leave.

"Of, of course, Your Majesty." Haman bowed and quickly let himself out.

Much to his surprise, he had not gotten far from the king's chambers before he was met by one of the king's chamberlains bearing the apparel and the crown he had just mentioned. The horse was already saddled and awaiting him. Haman was sure he saw a smirk pass over the face of the servant who handed the horse off to him, yet it was not evident enough for him to make a valid accusation.

Haman took the garments, the crown, and the horse that was offered him. Stalking toward

the king's gate, he could not believe what he was
about to do.

Chapter 15
A Twist of Fate

Mordecai inwardly sighed. He could see by the way Haman approached that he was on a mission. Although Mordecai expected a smile to be stretched over the evil man's face as he hastened to collect him for death, that was not quite the expression he was getting. It was an expression of hatred, which he had grown used to seeing each time he and Haman had an encounter, but also an expression of shame. Was Haman, somewhere deep inside his cruel heart, ashamed for the actions he was about to take? Was he ashamed for the seventy-five foot gallows he had erected overnight in order to hang Mordecai? Was he ashamed that he was allowing his hatred and rage for one man to justify eradicating an entire race of people? God alone knew the dark heart of Haman, and Mordecai was not about to waste any more effort trying to figure it out.

Whatever the reason for the look on his face, Mordecai was quite sure his time on earth was about to cease. He noticed how the crowd around him began to thin as Haman drew nearer. He did not blame the people, but he would not put up a useless fight. He had followed the path Jehovah had set before him, and he felt as if His God was pleased with his efforts. If the time had come for him to die, he would not fight it.

However, as Haman continued to approach, Mordecai could not help but wonder what it was that Haman carried with him? And why was he leading the king's steed behind him? Probably to mount and then use to drag Mordecai through the streets to the gallows. As Haman finally came upon Mordecai, he refused to look him in the face.

"By order of His Royal Majesty, King Ahasuerus. Mordecai, the Jew, shall be this day adorned with the royal garments of the king, bear the royal crown upon his head, and be led through the streets of the city upon His Majesty's royal steed." Haman's voice caught and his eyes shot fire in the direction of the man to whom he spoke. Haman cleared his throat to continue and extended the garments to Mordecai. As he took them from Haman, Mordecai could not help but notice the way Haman was shaking in pure rage and fury at being commanded to do this.

"You will be led through the city streets by myself, the king's most noble prince, and honored for your bravery and dedication to our Most Noble King, King Ahasuerus." Haman's voice shook in an effort not to break again under the stress of what he was saying.

Mordecai accepted the garments and the crown but had to stifle the smile that threatened his lips. He thought over the irony which was taking place at this very moment. The king had allowed Haman to write a decree that every Jew in the nation be slaughtered, yet this same king had instructed Haman to lead a Jew through the city streets, wearing not only his royal attire but also his royal crown while riding on his royal steed to show his delight to honor him.

Of course, it made sense now. Haman had not told the king it was the Jewish people he wished to destroy. He had simply told the king that there were certain people who considered their laws diverse from all the others, and that they chose to honor their laws over the laws of the king. Otherwise, King Ahasuerus would never allow a Jew to be honored in such a way.

Mordecai made a decision at that moment to accept the honor bestowed upon him, but not to gloat in it. Damage was most definitely being inflicted to Haman's pride at having to honor the man he so publicly hated in such a way. To gloat in that fact would make Mordecai seem as cruel as Haman. If Haman could only see past his anger, he would see that he, too, was being honored. After all, he had said the king commanded "his most noble prince" to lead the procession. That he had commanded Haman to do just that proved he was bestowing an honor upon Haman as well. His pride just would not allow him to see it.

Mordecai draped himself in the robe provided him and placed the crown securely upon his head. He half expected Haman to tease the horse as he mounted it, but he just stood there, face downcast, and awaited him to get into position. Once Mordecai was atop the steed, Haman begin to lead him through the city streets. People cheered as Haman continued to announce, *"Thus shall it be done unto the man whom the king delighteth to honour!"*

Up they went through the city streets, down the alleyways, and back through adjoining streets until they once again reached the king's gate. Mordecai slid from the back of his mount, removed the crown from his head, the robe from his back, and handed everything back to Haman. Once pats on the back were finished from on-lookers, he regained the same position in which he was before Haman had arrived that morning.

Haman used his own robe to cover his head and flee to his home, shame and disgrace evident with each step closer he drew to his threshold. He could not believe he had been disgraced in such a way! Mordecai. Any man but Mordecai! The worst part was, that everything he had done, every honor bestowed upon that despicable Jew, was a direct result of an idea he himself had shared with the king! He thought he was to be the man the king delighted to honor! He was supposed to be the one being led, not the one doing the leading!

"Zeresh!" he bellowed as he crossed through the door to his home. "Zeresh, where are you? Zeresh, my wife! Come to me! Comfort your grieving husband. You've no idea at the ridicule and dishonor I have had to endure this day! Zeresh, where are you?" Zeresh slowly rounded the corner and began to approach her husband who was purely wallowing in despair.

"Actually," she spoke matter-of-factly, "I do."

Haman, so distraught in his misery, did not realize she had spoken. He took her small hands into his larger ones and led her to be seated with him. "Sit with me, my love. I must share with you my despair. I went to speak with the king, to beg for permission to hang the man I so hate, but instead of hanging him from the gallows, I ended up being forced to bestow the king's honor on that very man. I had to lead him through the streets of the city. He was upon the king's steed, Zeresh, and wore the king's garments. He even bore the crown, Zeresh. The crown!"

"Yes, Haman. As I said, I know." He removed his hands, which were now covering his eyes and looked at his wife for some explanation. "Memucan and Tarshish are here," she continued nonchalantly. "They are dining in the main hall at the moment. They were in the city where you began the procession and could not wait to come tell me all about it." Her sarcastic smile showed the embarrassment she bore at being his wife at the moment. Haman looked at his wife in shock.

127

She already knew? She knew the shame he had been commanded to endure, yet she was not there to greet him at the door as he entered their home in his misery. He had to call for her repeatedly and then force her to sit and listen to him while his two "friends" sat and dined in luxury in his main hall!

"You already knew?" he questioned her.

"Yes, Haman. I already knew, and all I have to say is, I do not know what you were thinking." Zeresh stood, throwing her hands into the air as if he were insane. She could not have surprised Haman more had she stricken him across the face.

"I had to, Zeresh! The king commanded that he be honored. I had no choice in the matter. What was I supposed to say? Of course, Your Majesty, I'll honor him all the way to the gallows I had built for him, and then I shall be honored myself if you will allow me to hang him thereon!" Haman watched this woman in disbelief. What did she expect of him?

"No, Haman, I know why you honored him. I understand you had no choice in the matter as far as that was concerned, but mark my words, husband, from what has transpired this day, if Mordecai is of the Jews which you have planned to slaughter, you will not prevail against him. You will surely fall before him."

Haman sat and stared at his wife in utter disbelief. Everything that had transpired up to this point had been her idea. Hers and his closest friends. Surely she had been sampling the wine during her meal.

"Tarshish! Memucan! Bring yourself hither at once!" Haman did not bother to civilly send a servant after the friends he knew were still inside his home but yelled for them across the rooms of the large house. He heard a bit of ruckus from the other room and presently Tarshish arrived having not even bothered to put down the turkey leg he was currently enjoying. Memucan was not far behind him, goblet full of ale in hand.

"You ran straight to my home and told my wife of my misfortune," Haman spoke slowly to make sure his friends well understood what he was saying. "You now feast upon my food and drink my ale. Have you nothing of worth to say to me during this troubling time?"

Tarshish took a bite of his turkey leg and looked to Memucan. Memucan took a long drink from his goblet and looked to Haman. "I know not exactly what has happened to bring the current events into play, Haman, but after the events which we bore witness to today, I am quite certain you are in some serious trouble, my friend."

"Mordecai has found favor with the king, Haman," Tarshish continued around a bite of his turkey leg. "Why all of this took until now to come out, I know not, but one thing is for sure, King Ahasuerus will not take kindly to the slaying of the man whom he honored so publicly this day."

Zeresh stood gazing out the window as the men continued to speak openly with her husband. As she turned again to face them, the despair she saw upon Haman's face caused her a bit of sadness, yet, not enough to stop her from voicing her next questions. "Haman, when you spoke to the King about writing the decree to kill the "unlawful citizens" of the country, did you tell him it was the Jews you wished to kill? Did he understand that Mordecai was to be of that lot?"

"Specific names were not given," he answered her, "but do not try to turn all of this on me! The three of you were the ones to suggest I go to the king to begin with! You desired to see our family prosper as much as I did! The house of Haman will rise again, Zeresh, tell me you do not remember us having that very conversation!"

Haman was on his feet awaiting her answer, but before a word could utter from her lips, a knock sounded urgently at his door. It was not fast enough, however, to hide the nonchalant look on her face or the shrug of her shoulders.

"Prime Minister Haman!" the voice sounded from outside. "I have been sent to collect you immediately on order from His Majesty, King Ahasuerus!"

"The banquet!" Haman remembered aloud as he, himself, rushed to open the door.

Harbonah stood just outside, evidence of his run from the palace on his red face. "The king requests your presence immediately, sir. The feast has been prepared and the king and his queen anxiously await your arrival in order to begin." Harbonah took a deep breath to try and gain control of his breathing.

Haman turned to look at the wife he was no longer sure he knew and the men he had considered, until today, his closest friends. Without a word, he turned on his heels and slammed the door.

Chapter 16
Revelation

The king and queen sat in comfortable silence awaiting the arrival of Haman. Esther was silently praying, petitioning Jehovah for wisdom in the words she was about to deliver. The king, again, thinking to himself what a fool he had been to allow business to interfere in his relationship with the woman seated across from him.

She looked positively radiant this day. Esther had chosen a deep green gown, which she had learned was another of the king's favorite colors, accented with gold embroidery along the bodice and the sleeves. Her hair was once again pulled away from her face, this time into a smooth bun on the back of her head. Soft ringlets framed her beautiful face. Gold and emerald jewelry accented her head, neck, and wrists while a gold colored cape hung from her slender shoulders.

"I do apologize, My Queen, for the delay. I cannot imagine what is keeping Haman. He has always been so punctual be......" before King Ahasuerus could finish his sentence, Haman came hastily into the room.

Bowing as low has his body would allow, he began by profusely apologizing to the royal couple in front of him. "My King, My Queen, please accept my most humble apologies. An extremely urgent business matter arose right as I was about to depart. I pray for your mercies and forgiveness at my delinquency."

The king looked to his queen who gave him a subtle smile. "Shall we dine then?" he announced as he rose from his seated position, holding out his arm, which Esther graciously accepted. Haman could hardly believe he had been totally ignored. He supposed his apology was accepted, otherwise the king would have had him banished from the banquet. Scoffing at the royal couple behind their backs, he waited until they had both been seated before he made his entry into the dining hall.

As in the previous day, the meal went by quickly. Esther and the king exchanged light conversation, but unlike the previous day, Haman hardly uttered a word unless he was directly spoken to. Esther wondered what caused his silence. Just yesterday, she and the king had hardly been able to get a word in for Haman's mindless chatter.

At last the moment Esther was fearing was upon her and the time for the king and

Haman to depart had come. Again, the king looked to his queen to voice his question. This time, he took her hands in his as he looked into her eyes.

"I thank you for yet another glorious feast, My Queen. Yet again, I must ask. *What is thy petition, Queen Esther? and it shall be granted thee: and what is thy request and it shall be performed, even to half of the kingdom.*" Haman sat in the silence as eager as his king to hear her answer. He could not believe that yet again, a total now of THREE times the king had offered this woman up to half his kingdom! No king had ever offered a queen even half that much. But, if that is what she had wanted, she would have taken it after his first offer. What in the world did she want?

Esther did not try to stop the tear which slid down her cheek, nor the ones which followed. The time for silence had passed. She was not sobbing, but it was difficult to keep from doing so as she began to speak her next words to the king. Instead, she kept her voice calm as the tears slid slowly down her face. She felt the king's grip tighten around her fingers as he witnessed her tears, and then she began to speak.

"*If I have found favour in thy sight, O King, and if it please the king, let my life be given me at my petition, and my people at my request: For we are sold, I and my people, to be destroyed, to be slain, and to perish.*"

Haman closed his eyes as his world began to spin. He had never imagined this coming.

135

Clearly the king was still confused by what the queen was telling him, but Haman knew. He knew exactly. Esther was a Jew—one of the very Jews he had just vowed to slaughter. It all began whirling through his mind at an alarming speed. It all made sense now. Mordecai had presented Esther to the Court of the Women before the king had selected his queen. Esther had continually sought out Mordecai during public appearances. He was not just a friend to her. He was one of her people!

"My Queen, of what do you speak?" King Ahasuerus noticed how tightly Esther clung to his hands. It was if she was holding onto him for her very life.

"If we had been sold for bondmen and bondwomen, I would have kept my peace and held my tongue. I would have accepted the laws set for my people and myself, but I must petition you, My King, to spare me and to spare my people."

"Spare your life? Who? Who is he?" King Ahasuerus jumped to his feet in an all-out rage. "Where is he who plans to take your life!?!" Esther expected him to be alarmed, but even she was surprised at his outburst.

Esther slowly turned her head and locked eyes with Haman for what seemed like an eternity. King Ahasuerus caught the exchange and looked from his queen to the man he had trusted with not only his own life, but with his kingdom as well.

"No. No, My Queen, I had no idea," Haman began to shake his head in defiance.

The king felt his blood rush to his head, though it felt as if it had settled in his stomach as he looked from the women whom he so deeply loved, to his second-in-command, and back again.

"The adversary and enemy is this wicked Haman," Esther proclaimed as she pointed straight to the man who was continuing to protest the accusation.

"Your Majesty, I had no idea. I knew not the queen was of Jewish origin. You know I intended no harm toward her!"

King Ahasuerus felt as if his ears were about to burst. He had to get out. He had to comprehend these things he had just seen and heard. His mind was muddled, his world spinning. He looked over his shoulder and saw that Ja'al, Sayyid, and Harbonah, were all present right outside the room. Feeling sure the queen was safe in their presence, he said not a word as he rushed from the room and straight out into the palace garden to clear his head and think on the things which had been told to him.

How could he have been so stupid! Sinking onto a bench in the midst of the garden, he took a few breaths to calm his nerves, and thought back over the past months. His queen. His wife. The woman he had fallen deeply, madly in love with, was a Jew. The king had no problem with the Jews. He did not understand their religion, but they were good citizens of the country. They were a peaceful people who paid their taxes, and as long as his laws did not interfere with the laws of their God, they upheld the laws set before them by the king.

"That is it," the king said aloud, realization dawning on him. King Ahasuerus had noticed how power hungry Haman had become. He had heard his chamberlains jest at how many times a day Haman would walk through the city streets just to see people bow to him. When Haman had come to him speaking of "a certain people" who were "scattered abroad and dispersed," he had no idea he meant a certain "race" of people.

Haman hated the Jews because they would not worship him—Mordecai in particular. Mordecai always bowed to the king if he passed by or appeared before him, but it was a bow of respect, not a bow of worship as Haman demanded. So to gain complete vengeance on Mordecai, Haman declared to slaughter the entire race of his people. Haman had tricked him. Haman had tricked him into trusting him and by doing so had earned the right to rid the world of people he wanted revenge upon. And he, the King, had allowed it. He had allowed Haman to bear his signet ring.

King Ahasuerus ran his hand through his hair in utter defeat. How could he have been so stupid? This would not come to pass. Haman would lay not one hand on his queen or on any Jew as far as he was concerned! The king was back on his feet and running back toward the queen's chambers before another thought could pass through his head. He would not allow Haman to take her life! She was his, and he would protect her if his own life depended upon it!

King Ahasuerus had not gotten clear of the room before Haman was on his knees before the queen. Esther turned her face from him and refused to look him in the eye.

"My Queen, I beg of you. I had no idea you were Jewish!" he cried.

Esther said not a word but fled quickly from the room. Assuring the chamberlains she just need some time alone, she ran straight to her private chambers. She had to get away from him. She would hide herself until the king returned. She would hide and pray. Pray to Jehovah for continued guidance in dealing with the events which would transpire and pray for peace in whatever those events may be.

She had no doubt won the king's affection, and in truth, she had grown to love him, too. She could only pray that love would be enough to save herself and her people from the awful fate set before them. She knew that Jehovah could work miracles. She had allowed Him to lead her this far. She was not about to give up on her faith now. She just needed some time with Him. Time to cry out to Him and ask for more direction and more wisdom.

What Esther did not realize as she made her way into her private chambers was that Haman had gotten by the chamberlains and followed her there. He had acted as if he were leaving the palace, then doubled backed and arrived in Esther's rooms, unannounced. As she stretched herself out onto her bed to cry openly and freely to Jehovah, she was alarmed to feel such sudden pressure fall across her body. Her cry of alarm barely crossed her lips before her mouth was stifled.

"Please, My Queen!" Haman spoke for her ears alone. The crazed look in his eyes frightened her as he turned her to face him. "You can fix this. Tell the king I did not mean to cause you harm. Reassure him I had no idea you were a Jew! He will listen to you and give you what you desire! Spare my life, My Queen!"

Esther struggled free and a long scream pierced the air. "Get away from me you wicked man!" she cried. Esther was continuing to struggle to remove Haman from across her bed as the king and his chamberlains burst through her door.

"What is the meaning of this!?!" King Ahasuerus yelled. "Will he force the queen also before me in my house?" The king grabbed Haman by the shoulder and flung him from his wife's bed.

"My King! It was my wife, Zeresh, who convinced me to destroy Mordecai! It was she who insisted I kill the Jews!" Immediately, two chamberlains grabbed Haman's arms and covered his head with a sack, while he continued to scream and beg for mercy.

The king instantly had Esther in his arms, pulling her to himself as he tried to calm her frantic heart.

"Behold, My King," Harbonah spoke, "the gallows, seventy-five feet high, which Haman had planned to hang Mordecai upon, the same Mordecai you honored just today, stands at the house of Haman."

The king watched Haman struggle with the chamberlains while continually begging for his life. He knew Haman was blinded by the sack covering his head, but his hearing was still unhindered, except for his own constant groveling. Still, the king spoke his next words loud and clear to make sure there was no mistake to Haman who it was who spoke them.

"Hang him thereon," the king said slowly, emphasizing each word clearly.

"As you command, My King," Harbonah acknowledged as he motioned to the others to lead Haman away.

"Wait!" the king spoke as he arose from his place with the queen. He walked to Haman, whose head was still covered and took his hand in his own. "I'll be needing this," he commented as he removed his signet ring from the hand of his now enemy.

"Sire," Harbonah spoke, and in an instant, they were gone.

The king returned to Esther's side and settled onto the bed beside her. He wrapped his arm around her pulling her close to him, waiting for her breathing to return to normal and her tears to abate. Finally, she began to calm.

"I am so sorry, my love, that you have had to endure such a tragic day. Continue to calm and refresh yourself, then meet me in my chambers within the hour?" It was a question. Not a command.

"As you wish, My King," Esther agreed. She tried to smile up at him, but it was almost too momentous a task at the moment. He gently kissed the top of her head, then left her in the capable hands of her lady-in-waiting and dearest friend, Sophia.

Chapter 17
Realization

King Ahasuerus walked slowly to his private chambers. He knew what he was about to do was unheard of, but he needed a moment to himself. As he approached the doorway to his room, he turned to the chamberlains who had escorted him there. Laying a hand on each of their shoulders, he made a simple command.

"Hatach, Ja'al," he spoke to each of them. "Take a turn about the palace. I require a moment solely on my own."

"But, Sire, your safety..." Ja'al began.

"I am safe," the King assured them. "The enemy you had the power to protect me from, has been destroyed. Sayyid and Yusuf are stationed right outside my outer doors. No harm will come to me. I simply need some time, completely alone, to collect my thoughts before my queen arrives."

"Yes, Your Majesty," the men spoke and bowed in unison then exited the hallway as the king let himself into his room.

Settling on the edge of his bed, now that he was sure he was completely and utterly alone, he allowed his own tears to spill. He had spoken truthfully to his chamberlains. The enemy they could have protected him from was swinging from the gallows that same enemy had built himself. However, the enemy they could not protect him from, the enemy who was more of a danger to the king than Haman ever would have been, was he, himself.

Again he questioned how he had been so easily blind-sided. He had almost lost her. If Esther would not have come forth and told him all that was transpiring, it would have been her lovely neck swinging from the gallows in just a few short months, and he would not have even realized it was happening. How could he have been so ignorant?

The king slid from the side of his bed and onto his knees, his tears coming in a torrent now. Laying his head upon his bed, he thought about the careless and unethical way he had been ruling his kingdom. He thought of the blood-thirsty man he once was. He thought of the families he had ruined, demanding their men fight, to create a better country, only to have created orphans and widows as he returned home without a victory. He thought of the evil things he had done and demanded of Vashti when she was still his queen.

At one point, the king stopped and raised his head asking himself what he had become? He quickly dried his tears and quieted his sobs. He had never been such a soft-hearted fool before, but that was before he had met and given his heart to the woman who now held the title of his queen. This woman had changed him. She had changed who he was, what he was, and what he wanted to become.

That thought alone threatened more tears, but he held himself in check. What agony must she have endured the past weeks. He had not called for her in over a month, yet she was still as kind and receiving of him as she always had been. And that was after she had learned that a decree had been signed in his name to destroy herself and her entire race of people.

He had no idea his queen was a Jew. He had no idea it was the Jews whom Haman had intended to destroy. But still, she came to him in a calm and loving manner to plead with him to spare not only herself but her people as well. She was not ranting and raving as she could have been but was humble and respectful.

A deep sigh was the only noise Esther heard as she approached the king's door. She had asked Sayyid to allow her to enter unannounced, hoping their relationship was maturing to that level, and because the king was already expecting her, Sayyid had allowed it. However, now may not be the time to test those waters. Esther backtracked and asked Sayyid to announce her after all.

Sayyid agreed without question and quickly knocked on the door to the king's chambers. Esther could not be certain, but she was sure she heard another sigh and perhaps a sniffle before the king bade her enter.

"My King," she bowed before him. "Allow me to again extend my gratitude to you for sparing my life at the hands of Haman. I know he was your most trusted advisor and friend, but…" Esther's voice broke and the king was instantly at her side.

"Enough, My Queen," he spoke as he pulled her to him. "I had no idea of the true nature of Haman, or perhaps I did but simply failed to see. None the less, you are my wife and my queen. Your safety is of more importance to me than the life of anyone who threatens that, regardless of whom they may be."

He released her from his embrace but kept her hand in his and led her to the balcony off his bedchamber. They stood for a moment in silence before the king began to speak.

"Esther," he began slowly. "I must confess that I had no idea you are Jewish." He saw the fear that crossed her features and quickly rectified his statement. He did not wish her any more stress or fear this day. "However, it is not a fact that disturbs me," he quickly assured her. "I hope you realize that our relationship has evolved to the point that it would take much more than your religious preferences to deter me."

"I hoped you felt that way, Sire. However, it had been so long since you had sent

146

for me, I confess I had begun to fear that I had lost favor in your eyes, though for what cause I could not comprehend."

The king looked over his kingdom and watched as people came and went from the palace gates. He knew many were gathered near the gallows where the execution of Haman had just taken place. "I admit, reflecting over the past few weeks, you had every right to feel that way. It seems Haman had me blind-sided in more areas than one. I feel he was keeping me from you intentionally, at least on several occasions when he knew I planned to call for you. You see, Esther, I am different around you. I am not the man I was before we were married. I view things differently than I did before. I fear Haman was not pleased with the king he felt I was becoming—more of a pacifist than a man of war, not unwilling to fight if need be, just not as willing to jump into battle and suffer loss."

Esther was not sure he was still talking to her. His mind seemed afar off. Truly he had endured loss this day. His second-in-command and trusted friend had been revealed as a treacherous liar who only sought out his own personal advancement. She must work to comfort him as well.

"Men often disappoint, Your Majesty. That is why Mordecai always taught me not to put any one person too high on a pedestal for they will surely fall. Look to none for perfection, except Jehovah."

"Mordecai taught you these things?" He was definitely back with her now.

"Yes, My King. My parents died when I was very young and Mordecai took me to raise as his daughter. In actuality, he is but a cousin, but in my heart he is much more. He is now my earthly father."

Esther was surprised at how easy it was to, at last, reveal these things to the king. And she was surprised at the weight that lifted from her heart as she bore the truth to him.

"Mordecai, the very Mordecai which I bestowed honor upon just today, is your father?" The king had a handsome smile on his face at the realization. Esther realized how much she had missed that smile.

"Yes, for all intents and purposes," she laughed. "The same."

Esther watched in wonder as he quickly left the balcony and almost ran to the doors where his chamberlains stood at arms.

"Yusuf, Sayyid!" he called to them.

At once their attention was directed to their King. "Yes, Your Majesty," they said in unison.

"Seek out Mordecai at once and bring him in haste. I require an audience with him immediately! Make him comfortable in the throne room and notify me upon his arrival." The king's voice was stern yet kind.

"As you wish, Sire," Yusuf acknowledged exiting the main doors quickly.

The king returned to his queen's side on the balcony and took each of her hands in his own.

"Esther, Haman was your enemy and the enemy of your people which made him my enemy as well. However, his assault was directed toward the Jewish people. Because you have overcome that assault, through your wisdom and courage, Haman is dead. Therefore, all of his possessions are now yours. You will now rule over the house of Haman and will have the deciding factor on what is to become of his family."

Esther contemplated exactly what it was the king was giving her.

"Your Majesty," she began slowly, "before Haman was led away, he spoke of Zeresh, his wife, being the culprit behind his schemes. If that be the case, she is as evil and wicked as he. Do you believe that to be true?"

Ahasuerus thought for a moment. "Though the deeds Haman was charged with were clearly his own doing, it is true that Zeresh did not make life easy for him," he answered her truthfully. "She was always seeking for a way to increase his power, and by that, her place in society. I would not be surprised if her suggestions did not persuade Haman to act on the events which caused his demise. After all," the king looked to Esther and cast her a shy smile, "we all know the power of persuasion comes easily to beautiful women. Especially when directed toward the men who love them." The king finished his last sentence slowly and had focused his attentions upon her face.

Esther quickly lowered her head as she blushed to the roots of her hair. In the five years they had been married, this was the first the king had ever hinted at actually loving her.

Gently he lifted her chin until she had no choice but to look into his face. "I have never told you, Esther, I never spoke of it to Vashti or any of the other women whom I have been acquainted with. I have never spoken the words, because until now, they were never true. I love you, Esther. I have loved you from the first moment I laid eyes on you. But I can honestly say that I love you more today than I have ever loved anyone in my lifetime, and by tomorrow, my feelings toward you will have doubled, continuing to do so with each passing day, until I cease to breathe."

Esther's tears came freely again, but this time her tears were happy ones. She had not lost favor with her king. Better yet, the passion he felt for her was indeed more than physical attraction. She was about to pledge her heart to him as well, but a knock on the door inside his bedchamber interrupted them before she could find her voice. Quickly, she dried her tears as he gently placed his fingers across her lips.

"We shall continue this conversation," he smiled and quickly dropped a kiss upon her head before he bid the chamberlain to enter.

"Excuse me, Sire, but Mordecai has been made comfortable and is awaiting your arrival in the throne room as you requested."

"Thank you, Yusuf." Yusuf bowed and turned away. "My Queen." The king spoke as he offered Esther his arm. Graciously, she moved to accept, but not before she reached up and softly brushed her lips across his cheek. Now, it was the king's turn to blush.

Chapter 18
Saving Knowledge

It was a somber couple who made their way to the throne room. Upon arriving, Esther wasted no time in racing to Mordecai from the king's side. Mordecai, who had not even had a chance to hit his knees upon their sudden arrival, suddenly found himself engulfed in a fierce embrace by the woman he had raised from a child. Again, King Ahasuerus watched the passion upon Esther's face as she quickly approached and embraced one she loved, hoping he would one day warrant such a greeting.

"My Queen, My King," Mordecai bowed as he reluctantly pulled away from Esther's embrace. "I am honored to be asked into your presence."

"The honor belongs to the queen and I, Mordecai," the king spoke directly. "I have recently learned that it is once again you to whom I owe a debt of gratitude. Once I bestowed honor upon you for saving my life from my own chamberlains who sought to lay hands on me and physically harm me. Now I find I shall bestow honor upon you for saving my life from another enemy—myself. Haman sought to destroy you, and in turn he would have destroyed the one thing in my life that I have found matters to me more than my own." The king looked to his wife. "My queen."

He turned back to Mordecai and began to chuckle to himself. "Alas, the man who raised a woman with such wisdom and courage certainly deserves a place inside the palace with her. I sincerely and personally thank you for setting her on the path as a mere child to become the Queen of Persia. She has changed me from the man I once was. Mordecai, from this day forward, it is you who shall be my second-in-command. You shall assist me in all matters of ruling my kingdom, offering me counsel, wisdom and at times, even instruction." The king was serious. Mordecai was speechless. Esther was breathless.

The king once again removed his signet ring from his hand, but this time he had given much thought prior to his actions and had complete assurance he was directing it to one who deserved it. "This ring holds the power to create and set forth laws and decrees that will be followed by all of Persia. Once this seal is applied, even I cannot reverse what it commands."

Mordecai slowly took the ring from the king's outstretched hand. "Your Majesty, I do not know what to say."

"Say nothing, Mordecai, save that you will excuse me for a few moments. I will return, for we have much to discuss. For the moment, Prime Minister Mordecai, My Queen, I must make sure the decisions I have made are recorded properly and immediately in the Chronicles, and, I feel the two of you deserve a few moments alone to become reacquainted after the events of the day."

Mordecai bowed to his king. Ahasuerus took his queen's hand and gently lifted it to his lips. "My Queen," he spoke as he slightly bowed in her direction. Esther curtsied low as he pressed a kiss gently on the back of her hand.

A sweet smile from his queen would suffice until their next meeting. He took his leave knowing Esther could not be any safer than she was at this moment. She was in the presence of the man who raised her, this man who was now his second-in-command, along with his most trusted chamberlains right outside the door.

Esther was once again welcomed into Mordecai's warm embrace. It was so good to see him again and now be able to acknowledge him as a part of her family and not just a dear, old man in the court.

"What an eventful day it must have been for you, my sweet Esther," Mordecai spoke, breaking the silence. "Are you well? I know the day's events have been trying."

Esther could see the concern deep in her cousin's eyes. "I am fine," she assured him, "a bit tired, but otherwise, I could not be better.

Mordecai, King Ahasuerus gave me command over the house of Haman. I am giving it to you. His possessions are yours, as well as the decision on what is to become of his family, whom I have learned had a strong hand in all the wrong-doings against our people." A radiant smile broke out across Esther's lovely face. "Oh Mordecai, can you believe how Jehovah has allowed all of this to transpire! We are saved, Mordecai! Haman is gone! There is hope for the Jewish people. And you, Prime Minister!" Esther's smile lit up her beautiful face, but soon faded as she took in Mordecai's stern expression. She could not understand why he was not as ecstatic as she over the recent events. He still seemed forlorn and concerned. Perhaps he was just overwhelmed.

"Mordecai? Is something wrong? Do you not wish to be second to the king?" The crease in her brow proved to Mordecai that she did not realize the situation regarding their people still raged out of control.

He led his queen, which was still in so many ways the sweet, little girl he had taken to raise, to the steps of the platform where the throne stood. Settling themselves upon the steps, he took her hands in his and looked deep into her eyes. There he saw uncertainty and fear, just as he had seen when her parents had died so many years before.

"My Queen." Mordecai did not wish to alarm her, but she did need to understand the severity of the situation which still remained. It reminded him of when he had to deliver the news to her that her parents were dead and that he was all she had left in the world. Nevertheless, he had to explain it to her. "I fear the Jewish people remain in grave danger," he began.

"But I do not understand," Esther interrupted him. "Haman is dead; his body swings from the gallows as we speak." Esther pointed to the window where the crowd was still gathered.

"But do you not remember the comment our king spake upon handing me this ring?" Mordecai handed the ring to Esther for her to view. "He said that once this seal is applied to a decree, even he has not the power to reverse what it commands." He paused to give his words time to take meaning. He watched her expression go from one of elation to one of despair.

"The decree to slaughter our people began with Haman, My Queen, but it did not die with him. And the king cannot do anything about it. Yes, you and I have hope, but I fear our people do not."

Esther began to shake her head profusely. "No, Mordecai. No. You must be wrong." Tears again began to well in her eyes.

"I wish I were, Esther, but I fear I am correct. We must find a way to rectify that which has been written if we are to save our people from their demise."

Esther stood to her feet and began to pace the confines of the throne room. She had come too far to lose her faith. "Jehovah," she began to silently plead, "please, show me the path you would have me take. Give me an answer, Lord. Instruct me how to save my people," she cried as she sank to her knees. Mordecai bowed with her and placed his arms around her slender shoulders. The steps to the throne became their altar, and together they prayed that Jehovah would show them how to save their people when it seemed more impossible now than ever.

This was how Ahasuerus found them, huddled together on their knees in tearful prayer to their God. He was not sure what to say, or if he should say anything at all. At first, he thought they were thanking their God for delivering them from the gallows. However, as he moved closer, he realized their prayers were more of a desperate plea than a prayer of thanksgiving. Not knowing exactly how to proceed, but not wishing to continue to eaves drop, he did what he was used to doing in situations he was not sure how to control. He approached his throne. There he felt confident and in control, regardless of how any situation around him was unfolding.

The couple who were bowed before him did not realize they had been joined by their king. As he stepped around them and settled in his place upon his throne, he softly cleared his throat. The noise was enough of a distraction that Mordecai looked up to see the king watching them with confusion.

"Sire," he exclaimed, slowly raising from his knees and retreating from the platform steps.

Esther raised her head, but did not stand. She remained at his feet as she begged for his mercy. "Your Majesty," she cried, "please, please save my people. Please find a way to put away the mischief and deceit of Haman the Agagite and his treacherous and murderous plan against the Jews." The king's heart broke at once again seeing her face streaked with her tears, tears he could have prevented had he been more observant of those he empowered.

What he *desired* to do was grab hold of her, kiss her until they were both breathless, and promise her no Jew, or any other she desired, would ever be harmed as long as he were king. Anything to end her suffering. What he *could* do, however, was a different story. He knew he was powerless against the decree Haman had implemented.

At a loss for words, he held out his scepter to Esther, bidding her to stand. She did so, wiping at the tears streaking her face. Rising, she stood before him, calmed herself and once again, assumed the stance of a queen.

"Your Highness," she sniffled, "*If it please the king, and I have found favor in his sight, and the thing seem right before the king, and I be pleasing in his eyes, let it be written to reverse the letters devised by Haman the son of Hammedatha the Agagite, which he wrote to destroy the Jews which are in all the king's provinces.*" Esther paused to attempt to gather herself before she again lost control of her emotions. However, this proved harder than she thought as she struggled to continue. "*For how can I endure to see the evil that shall come unto my people? Or how can I endure to see the destruction of my kindred?"* Her voice broke and another tear, tears which she thought she was able to control, slid along her cheek.

Mordecai was not sure if he were overstepping the boundaries of his new title or not, but he could not bear to be separate from his daughter a moment longer. Slowly he approached her and placed a supportive arm about her waist. He did not want the king to feel she was alone in her endeavor to save their people. Just because she was safe and just because he was safe, did not mean their plight for freedom was over.

Few times in his life had Ahasuerus been without words. However, this was one of those times. He had not given another thought to the Jews once he knew his queen was safe. But clearly this remarkable woman in front of him was not satisfied simply with her own well-being or even that of her father. She truly cared for the other Jews scattered about his vast province, some of whom she did not even know. She never failed to impress him with her deep compassion and tender heart. She was so much more a queen to the people than he a king.

The king thought to himself. He was powerless over the decree, but perhaps there was hope for the Jewish people yet. As much as he had given his ring thoughtlessly to one who craved violence and revenge before, he had now given his ring to one who sought peace and prosperity for those same people. Looking at the couple in front of him, a smile broke across his features.

"My Queen," he began, "though I am powerless over the decree as it stands, dry your tears. There is hope for your people, yet. Mordecai," he continued as he looked to the man who now bore that ring, "I have given Esther the house of Haman, and he has been hanged upon the gallows because he laid his hand upon the Jews. You bear the ring which set that decree into effect. Write ye also for the Jews, as it liketh you, in the king's name and once sealed with the king's ring, no man may reverse."

At once, peace filled Esther. She had been so distraught that she had not been thinking clearly. Mordecai held the ring! Though he could not change that which had been written, he held the power to rectify the situation!

"Mordecai, is there time? Can a new decree be written which will give the Jewish people a hope, a chance to defend themselves perhaps?" Esther knew she was pleading, but she was pleading for the lives of her people.

"It will be difficult to write the decree, have it translated as needed, and get it to each corner of the empire in the short amount of time which remains, but Jehovah knows no boundaries, My Queen. We shall do all we can to save our people and leave the rest to the Almighty." Mordecai gave her waist a squeeze and looked to the king. "Your Majesty, I will need scribes and men to deliver the commandment."

The king acknowledged Mordecai's request with a simple tilt of his head. Then after ordering his chamberlain to summon and bring forth the scribes, he looked again to Mordecai and his queen.

"Whatever you need, you must simply speak. I will do all in my power to correct that which has been unjustly brought upon your people," he assured them.

"Then perhaps, My King, now is a good time for us to speak with you about the power of prayer," Esther simply stated.

King Ahasuerus looked at his wife. Never had he served anyone but himself, but after the events of the past months, and looking further back over the events of the time since she had become his queen, perhaps she was right. There was a greater power involved than that which he alone possessed.

"Very well," he stated. "Teach me of prayer and of the Jehovah to whom you pray. Too much has transpired for me to simply accept it as coincidence. I am willing to accept that my actions have done nothing but bring heartache and despair to those I love. Perhaps there is One who can accept me and lead me in the path of righteousness. You both have overcome much. Much of which I am responsible for. I cannot pretend you have done so alone."

Esther reached for the hand of her king. He was slow to respond, but he was sincere. Reaching out to take her hand, the king rose from his throne and together the three of them bowed upon the steps of their altar and prayed for guidance, instruction, and wisdom for the days ahead.

Chapter 19
Retaliation

The writing was complete and the decree sealed with the king's ring. Mordecai and Esther stood outside the palace gates and looked at the long line in front of them. True to his word, the king had spared no expense and had gathered the finest horsemen, as well as mules, camels, and dromedaries to carry the precious post across his vast empire.

Esther poured over the contents of the last letter before handing it off to the man who would carry it the greatest distance. She had to satisfy her mind once more, that the letter he bore was indeed the letter Mordecai himself had written, not one that had been somehow intercepted and rewritten. There she found the same familiar content as was in the previous letters:

By the command of King Ahasuerus, Jews in every city are to gather themselves together and to stand for their life, to destroy, to slay and to cause to perish all the power of the people and province that would assault them, both little ones and women. In doing so, they are free to take the spoil of them for a prey, upon the thirteenth day of the twelfth month.

Her people were being commanded to fight back on the very day Haman had commanded them to be slaughtered in cold blood, to stand up and defend themselves against any who would rally against them. The Jews would be ready to avenge themselves on their enemies, and as an added bonus for all that had been forced upon them, the Jews would be allowed to take the possessions of those they killed.

Esther folded the letter and placed it inside the leather pouch that would hang on the horseman's side. Handing it up to him, she gave him a slight smile with a plea in her eyes. "Ride safely and swiftly. Many lives depend upon it," she spoke to him.

"Yes, My Queen," he promised her bowing his head as he spoke.

Before the command to depart was given, the king stood before the men now mounted and situated upon their animals. The animals seemed as anxious as the men upon their backs to be on their way. The tension and importance of the load they carried seemed to hang in the air.

"The decree you carry is perhaps the most important decree in the history of my reign," the king began. "Nothing shall slow your pace until you arrive at your appointed destination. I have wronged many in my reign as king. I work every day to right those wrongs. You stood by me then, and I am commanding you to stand by me now. Do not fail me as you begin your journey. The lives of many depend on it." The king stepped from his place in front of the line and looked to Mordecai to give the final command.

"Godspeed, each of you!" Mordecai cried. He reached out to slap the haunches of the camel nearest him, which signaled all to venture forth as quickly as possible. Esther covered her mouth and nose as clouds of dust billowed around them. In what seemed like the blink of an eye, all that remained were those dust clouds, still lingering in the air behind them. Esther looked to her husband and Mordecai where they stood.

"Now?" she questioned.

"Send for the town crier," the king ordered his guard nearby. "The decree must also be read here at Shushan."

The weeks and months which followed were filled with both joy and anguish. Mordecai was clothed in royal apparel in blues and purples with jewels and crowns of gold bestowed upon him by Ahasuerus. The Jews in every province and every city were filled with gladness and rejoiced as the decree made its way across the empire. Feasting and dancing, rejoicing and massive celebrations were taking place all across the land.

Upon hearing the decree, many Persians begin to question their allegiance to one another, fearing they would be brought down by the Jews on the day which had been appointed. After all, the Jews now held great power in Persia. The queen and the king's second-in-command were each of Jewish descent, and Persians across the empire feared the control the Jewish people had been given. It was of no surprise that many of those Persians became Jewish followers based on their fear of the Jews, practicing their religion and standing with them in the face of scorn.

The anguish of the day came in not knowing who was ally and who was enemy. As Jews and Persians celebrated alike, each race contemplated who would be battling whom once the thirteenth day of the twelfth month approached. However, as more and more Persians converted to the Jewish belief, tensions eased and hearts and minds again became light and cheerful.

Esther had never been happier. Though she still feared the day of battle, she rejoiced in what had been done in an attempt to save her people. She and the king had never been closer, and he was constantly striving to learn more of her ways and the ways of Jehovah whom they served. Their relationship was on solid footing, and nights spent alone were long forgotten.

Sophia and Sayyid were granted permission from the king and were busy making plans for their wedding procession. Queen Esther was happy to be able to assist Sophia with her plans, and many days while the king and Mordecai discussed matters of business, Esther and Sophia were busy planning feasts and discussing matters of the heart. Sophia had been granted the use of the palace gardens in which the actual ceremony would take place, and the wedding procession would be one not soon forgotten.

Sayyid had been promoted to one of the king's chief chamberlains, and never had one man been more loyal to another. Since the king had mended his ways and sought peace with Jehovah, he, Sayyid and Mordecai spent many hours discussing their Maker and ways they could serve Him well.

The day, however, they all had been dreading was finally upon them. King Ahasuerus ordered Esther to her chambers and increased security in, as well as around, her quarters. Guards were stationed outside the doors which entered the actual rooms where she was to remain, as well as the entrance to her quarters and outside the windows. No one would get through to her without direct permission from himself, Mordecai, or Sayyid.

Everyone in Shushan and throughout the empire knew the king's stand on the decree. They knew that to fight against the Jews was to stand against the king. However, there were a few Persians in the midst who sought to avenge Haman's death. What better way to do so than to take down the two famous Jews who had turned the tables on him and had him hanged from the gallows? The king knew there was a significant threat to his second-in-command and to his queen, and those threats were not something he took lightly.

Esther paced the confines of her quarters. She dared to glance out her window from time to time, only to withdraw herself back at the plea of her lady-in-waiting.

"My Queen, please." Sophia begged her. "You must stay away from the window. The chamberlains below have no power against a well-aimed arrow. I could not live with myself should harm come to you."

"I know the Jews have made and are continuing to make their stand across this nation, as well as Persians who have sided with us. Yet, as this day draws to an end," Esther stopped pacing and looked to her friend and companion, "I confess that my heart is burdened with fear for those who have perished and for those who have lost their loved ones in this war—those who will never be as protected as I am now. Those who are, at this moment, continuing to face death at the hands of our enemies. And those who survive yet will endure ridicule and hate from this day forward, just because they are Jewish."

"My Queen," Sophia approached her quickly and smiled gentle reassurance to her. "You have always prayed for God to comfort you in times of despair. Let us go to Him now and ask for peace of mind and for continued safety of those we love."

Together they bowed there in the middle of the room and began to pray. Each of the ladies arose moments later with a calm assurance and with a peace that passeth all understanding, a peace neither could deny came from Jehovah alone.

They had only been risen for a moment when a knock was heard on the doors of the outer chambers. Each lady sought the comfort of the other as they heard exchanges being made to assure the guarding chamberlain that it was indeed an ally seeking entry. In but a moment, Sayyid was in the arms of Sophia as he came to report directly to the queen.

"Do you have news, Sayyid?" the queen questioned him as soon as he and Sophia's embrace was broken.

"News has traveled fast, My Queen. The Jews and their allies have stood strong against the Persians who sought to destroy them and have emerged in victory. I know the king is being briefed this moment of the happenings here, within the palace walls."

Hardly before Sayyid could finish his sentence, the king approached the queen's chambers. What happened next would be forever burned into the king's memory. He came to deliver her news of the number slain within the palace and to see what she had learned, but the greeting he received from his wife, was better than any news he could have delivered.

Upon seeing his entry, Esther rushed to him and threw her arms around his neck. It was the greeting he had so often hoped for, prayed for even, and now she was freely and openly expressing her gratitude at seeing him. Esther loved him. She loved him deeply and passionately. The fact that Mordecai was on his heels made the moment even sweeter, as she failed to break the embrace at Mordecai's approach. He cradled his wife in his arms, holding her to him with a force no man could match. It was a moment he would cherish even amidst the throes of war.

At last she broke her hold on him and almost flushed as she realized the display of affection she had shown in front of the others. The king determined not to allow her to experience embarrassment over her obvious joy at seeing him, proceeded with his reason for coming to her, while keeping his arms securely around her waist.

"The Jews have slain and destroyed five hundred men in Shushan the palace," he told her as he continued to hold her to his side. "Have you news of the other provinces?"

Esther looked to Sayyid. "Only that there has been victory over all the realm," she smiled softly to him.

"Very well," the king was pleased. "What now, My Queen?" he asked her. "What is thy petition, and it shall be granted thee? What is your request and it shall be done."

Suddenly a thought that could have come only from Jehovah crossed through Esther's mind. Just because the day in which the battle was declared to be fought had passed, did not mean the fight would. After all, five hundred men had sought to destroy her and Mordecai within the palace, knowing they would face the wrath of the king if they succeeded. Looking to her father and then to the king she spoke with clarity and wisdom once again.

"If it please the king, let it be granted to the Jews which are in Shushan to do tomorrow also according unto this day's decree." Slowly she finished her request, *"and let Haman's ten sons be hanged upon the gallows."* Esther knew that she had to show the Persians that Jews and their allies had control of the palace in order to have peace within their home. Apparently, just knowing the king's wrath would be upon them if they killed her and continued their fight with the Jews was not enough. Perhaps evidence of just how futile that wrath could be would send the message that the Jews were not to be trifled with.

The king looked to Sayyid. "Give the order, Sayyid. See that the bodies of Haman's sons swing from the gallows before nightfall."

"Yes, My King," he promised bowing and then exiting immediately to carry out the order.

Mordecai stepped up to speak to his king and queen. "Another thing being noted, is that our people refuse to take the spoils of those they kill. I believe that should show that our people are not killing to gain possessions, but only in defense of their lives."

173

"It seems that wisdom is something other Jews possess as well," the king smiled to his queen. "Let us retire for the evening, dear Esther," he said as he begin to lead her from her room. "You will be as safe in my chambers as you are in your own."

"Until tomorrow, Your Majesties," Mordecai bowed as they exited.

A moment later, Sophia and Mordecai smiled to one another as the sound of Esther's laughter floated through the hallway.

Chapter 20
Purim

As Esther had anticipated, more fighting broke out the following day, but only within Shushan. Three hundred more lives were ended as enemy fighters continued to attempt to gain access into the palace and destroy the queen and Mordecai. A useless attempt, for the Jews were ready for them and achieved another victory inside the palace walls. Again, the Jews refused to take possession of the goods of those they killed, knowing that to do so would make them appear greedy and self- serving.

However, Jews outside of Shushan were able to rest and enjoy their victory on this day. Their enemies had been defeated. They were once again respected by the Persians, regardless of their heritage and religious beliefs. Two of their own held positions of power inside the palace. It was a happy day for the Jewish people indeed and that was not something they took lightly.

Once the palace enemies were defeated, a feast to end all feasts began. King Ahasuerus declared a day of celebration, and Jews all over the province, rich and poor alike, celebrated their victory together. Gifts, food, and aid were bestowed upon all, as the entire race celebrated the mercy God had bestowed upon them.

At last Mordecai had his fill of celebrating and retired to his quarters for some quiet time with Jehovah. He bowed upon his knees and thanked God for His mercies, direction, and wisdom. He thanked Him for the position He had allowed him to achieve. He thanked Him for Esther and for entrusting her to his care when she was but a little girl and for the prudent and courageous queen she had become. Mordecai spent over an hour on his knees crying out his thanks to Jehovah and asking for direction on things that were sure to come. After an hour on his knees, the old man wiped the tears which streaked his face and rose slowly, taking into account the stiffness in his joints.

Making his way to his writing desk, he sat and begin to pen yet another decree to his people. This day shall be established, *the fourteenth day of the month Adar, and the fifteenth day of the same, yearly. As the days wherein the Jews rested from their enemies, and the month which was turned unto them from sorrow to joy, and for mourning into a good day: that they should make them days of feasting and joy, and of sending portions one to another, and gifts to the poor.*

A knock upon his door interrupted his writings, but it did not discourage him. Especially when he saw it was his queen who waited just beyond the portal.

"My Queen," he bowed upon opening his door. "Of what do I owe the pleasure of your visit this evening?"

Esther looked at this man she proudly considered her father and embraced his neck profusely. "I merely wish to thank you, Mordecai. Thank you for your guidance from my youth well into my adulthood and for the guidance you continue to bestow upon me now. Thank you for the prayers you continue to offer on my behalf—prayers that I can feel and know that come as petitions to Jehovah from you. I only hope to be a queen who will make you proud." Esther pulled away from him and looked into his tired and loving eyes. "I love you, Father Mordecai."

"And I love you, my sweet Hadassah," Mordecai returned, speaking her given name which she had not heard in over six years. Esther gently kissed his weathered cheek and turned to walk away. In the distance Mordecai saw the king awaiting his queen, a gentle smile upon his lips as he held up his hand in acknowledgement to his second-in-command. Mordecai returned the gesture of respect to his king, bowed his head slightly and closed the door as the royal couple ascended deeper into the palace, hand in hand.

The next morning, a decree was again sent to all the provinces in all the lands of Persia.

177

And the Jews undertook to do as they had begun, and as Mordecai had written unto them; Because Haman the son of Hammedatha, the Agagite, the enemy of all the Jews, had devised against the Jews to destroy them, and had cast Pur, that is, the lot, to consume them and to destroy them; But when Esther came before the King, he commanded by letters that his wicked device, which he devised against the Jews, should return upon his own head, and that he and his sons should be hanged on the gallows. Wherefore they called these days Purim after the name of Pur. Therefore for all the words of this letter, and of that which they had seen concerning this matter, and which had come unto them, the Jews ordained, and took upon them, and upon their seed, and upon all such as joined themselves unto them, so as it should not fail, that they would keep these two days according to their writing, and according to their appointed time every year; And that these days should be remembered and kept throughout every generation, every family, every province, and every city; and that these days of Purim should not fail from among the Jews, nor the memorial of them perish from their seed.

Esther and Mordecai smiled to one another as yet another decree was set into motion. This time, one of gladness. Their battle was won. Their reliance on Jehovah for direction, wisdom, and guidance had paid off. The celebration of Purim would always be a remembrance of the events which had transpired. Jewish people

178

everywhere would annually celebrate God's tender love and mercies toward His people, and by doing so, the young, Jewish girl would never be forgotten, whom God had brought from a homeless orphan to become *The Prudent Queen.*

Closing Thoughts

This book, *The Prudent Queen*, is an historical fiction account of Esther, Queen of the Persian Empire, but is based upon actual events. The unedited story of Queen Esther, can be found in the King James Version of the Holy Bible, however, this story was born in my imagination. One of my favorite Bible heroines of all time, Esther was a woman of whom I pray I gain a portion of her wisdom.

Although the Bible does not mention the salvation of King Ahasuerus, I cannot help but believe a man wise enough to choose Esther as his queen out of a province the size of his reign would be foolish enough to ignore the events which transpired and continue to turn away from God. Though I am not certain, I hope he is continuing to enjoy the company of Esther in heaven as we speak.

Sophia is a completely fictitious character by name, although the fact that Esther was granted chamber maids is not. Surely she became close to one over the others, a best friend so-to-speak, as women tend to do. I simply gave her a name and a simple love story all her own.

I hope you have enjoyed my story, and I encourage you to study the life of Esther and read her true story in the King James Version of the Holy Bible. It is a clear interpretation of how God is in charge of every situation at every moment and nothing ever surprises Him.

Another wonderful reference and study aid to the book of Esther is *Esther: Five Feasts and the Fingerprints of God* by Dr. Bo Wagner, available at www.wordofhismouth.com by Word of His Mouth Publishers.

Meet the Author

Angela was born and raised in the small town of Casar, North Carolina. Saved at the age of nine, she was taught by her parents to place her relationship with God before all others. She developed a love for writing at the age of six-years old, when she began keeping journals of her daily activities along with a notebook of her stories.

She was a member of the Young Writers Club at her middle school and a journalist for her high school newspaper during her Junior and Senior years. After high school, she continued her passion for writing by writing and directing Christmas and Easter plays at her home church.

She is an active member of Cornerstone Baptist Church in Mooresboro, North Carolina, where she attends with her husband John and their son Johnathan. A series of messages from Pastor Bo Wagner, was the inspiration she needed. After much encouragement from family and friends, she expanded her writing abilities to publish this, her first novel, *The Prudent Queen*.

Coming Soon

When Angels Speak

An historical fiction account of Mary, Mother of Jesus

Recently betrothed to a man she barely knows, Mary must face condemnation from her family and her town when she is visited by an angel who promises she will soon immaculately conceive and carry the Son of God. Always a humble and willing servant to Jehovah, Mary will face trials and persecution like no other woman has ever been asked to, nor has a woman since. Will her faith prevail as she agrees to carry out the task asked of her? Can Jehovah protect her from her fears of the unknown and from the wrath her soon to be husband is sure to feel when she confesses her secret? What else will unfold throughout the journey she is being led into, *When Angels Speak*?